Dangerous Song

Norma Rawlings

Norma E. Rawlings

Pen Press Publishers Ltd

Copyright © Norma Rawlings 2004

All rights reserved. No part of this publication
may be reproduced, stored in a retrieval system,
or transmitted in any form or by any means,
electronic, mechanical, photocopying, recording,
or otherwise, without the prior permision
of the publishers.

All the characters in this story are fictitional.
Any resemblance to real people, alive or dead
are purely coincidental.

First published in Great Britain
Pen Press Publishers Ltd
39-41 North Road
London N7 9DP

ISBN 1 904754 16 3

A catalogue record for this book is available
from the British Library

Other books by the author:
SLEEPING DOGS
SLEEPING DOGS II

Printed and bound in Great Britain

Cover design by Jacqueline Abromeit

DEDICATION

To Kristina.
For giving me beautiful twin granddaughters, who have brought so much joy to our family.

ACKNOWLEDGEMENTS

Joan and Attilio(Tony) MAZZONI for their information on Italy
The BELGRADE THEATRE, Coventry.
THE FAMILY RECORD CENTRE, Myddleton Street, London
THELMA WOODRUFF - friend and midwife
Margaret CRISP for her help as an ex air-stewardess
Elaine MASON for allowing me to use her photograph, as Lucy.

CONTENTS

CHARACTERS

Mark and Lucy-Ann MORRIS	A tour guide and his wife
Claudia MORRIS	Their twin daughter
Colette MORRIS (air stewardess)	Their other twin daughter
Attilio ROSSINI/Tony ROSS\	A singer
Attilio ROSSINIjnr./Leo DENVER\	Twin son of Attilio and Claudia
Claudio ROSSINI/Clay DENVER	Twin son of Attilio and Claudia
Lucy ROSSINI/HARRIS	Daughter of Attilio and Claudia
Valeria ROSSINI	Attilio's mother
Zia Maria	Attilio's aunt
Isabella ROSSINI	Attilio's sister
Bruno ROSSINI	Attilio's youngest brother
Flavio ROSSINI	Attilio's eldest brother
Paula ROSSINI	Flavio's wife
Lorenzo and Zeta ROSSINI	Flavio's children
Sergio ROSSINI	Attilio's middle brother
Florence ROSSINI	Sergio's wife
Anna and Mario ROSSINI	Sergio's children.
Max CORDER	Attilio's best friend in America
Rebecca LAWSON	Lucy's best friend
Bill HARRIS	Claudia's 2nd husband
Mark and Luke HARRIS	Twin sons of Bill and Claudia
Rachel HARRIS	Bill's sister aand best friend of Colette
Simon HARRIS	Bill's cousin and husband of Colette
Martin HARRIS	Son of Simon and Colette
Joyce DAVIS	Lucy's music teacher at school
Henry KENDAL	Lucy's English teacher at school
Maureen JAMES	Friend of Claudia
Rose WHITE	Friend of Claudia and Maureen
Mrs. JACKSON	Lucy's customer at the hairdresser's
Ricky KNIGHT	Lead singer at the Cropwell Theatre
Martin DAVIS	Lucy's agent and brother-in-law to Joyce

Sir John PHILLIPS	Musical Director and husband of Lucy
Lizbeth and Maybelle PHILLIPS	Twin daughters of John and Lucy
Carla	Their nanny
THE CAST OF "SCARLETTE"	
Andres BOND (pet monkey)	Melanie
Julia WHITE & Kay ARCHER	Sisters of Scarlette O'Hara
Winifred JONES	(Skinny Winnie) Nanny
Mick MORRISON	Rhett Butler
Christopher FELLOWS	Ashley Wilkes
Daniel DAY	Mr. O'Hara

SOMETHING TO THINK ABOUT...

We like to trace our ancestors
Be it right
Or be it wrong
But when we unearth
Secrets dark
We sing a dangerous song...

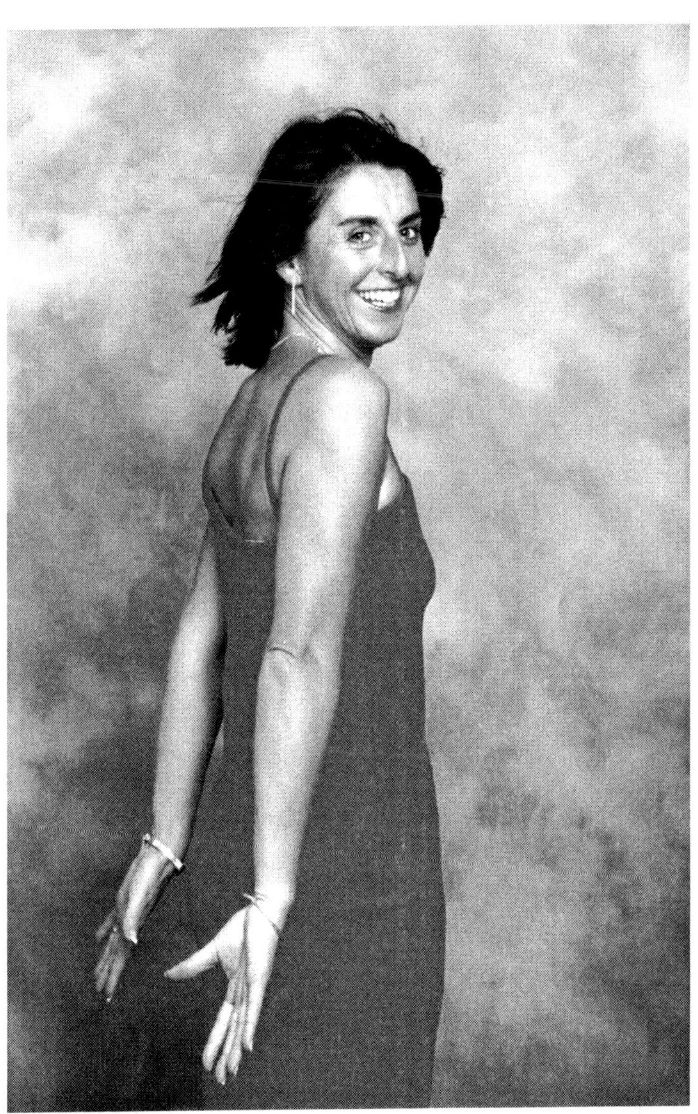

THE ROSSINI FAMILY

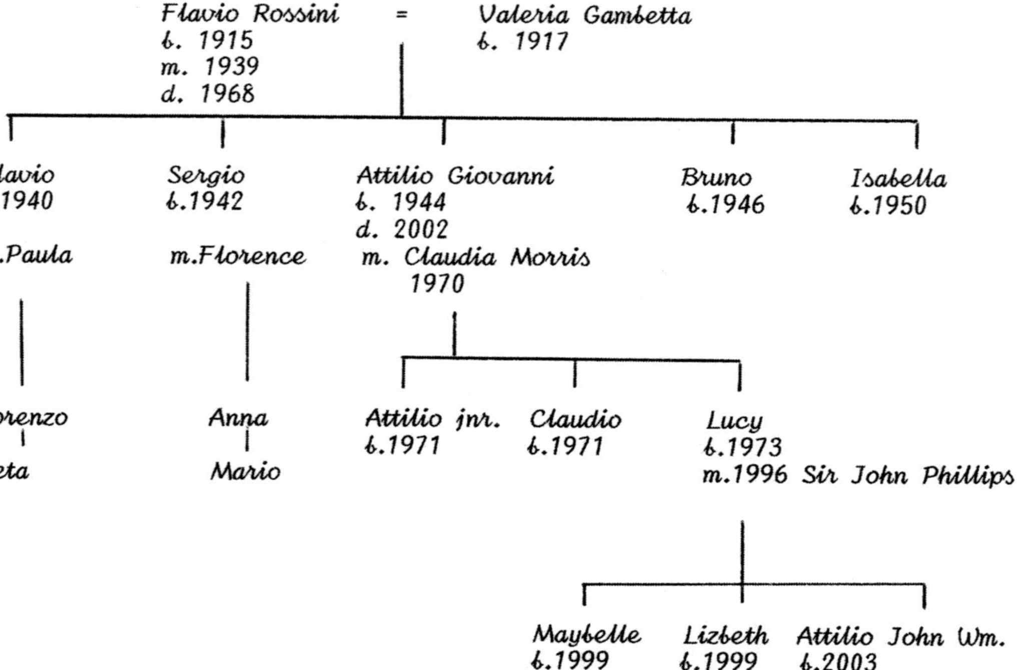

PROLOGUE

KITZBUHEL FEBRUARY 1970

"This is wonderful!"

"Come on. You're doing really well!"

"Right, I'll race you!"

"Hey, wait for me!"

They skied carefully down the nursery slopes, their eyes sparkling, their cheeks glowing.

The couple were having a wonderful time in Kitzbuhel in Austria. Mark Morris, tall, fair and athletic, was a tour guide, and as it was his wedding anniversary he had been allowed to bring his wife, Lucy Ann for a free holiday. A small dainty woman with light brown hair, she was enjoying every minute of it.

It was an idyllic day, with a bright winter sun shining down on a world of white, sparkling snow. Holidaymakers were zig-zagging down snowy slopes, or gliding up and down in cable cars, admiring the magnificent views. Others were sitting in bars eating, drinking and chatting away happily, while children were running about squealing and throwing snowballs. It was a winter wonderland.

The avalanche came without warning - a great tidal wave of snow, ice, boulders and broken trees, crushing everything in its path. It roared down the mountainside without mercy.

The air was filled with a white mist and the screams of terror as bewildered people watched death rushing towards them.

There were no survivors.

Two weeks later the bodies of Mark and Lucy Ann Morris were flown home to England.

ONE

LONDON TO MILAN 1970

The funeral was over - the guests had gone.

The two young women stood side by side looking desolately out of the window. It was growing dark and large snowflakes were fighting a losing battle against the heavy rain, which hammered onto the glass.

"I can't believe they're gone. Both of them together."

"Neither can I. It's too awful for words."

"Mum was having a wonderful time. She'd always wanted to learn to ski."

"I know. If it hadn't been their anniversary she wouldn't have gone."

"True. Perhaps it was fate that they should go together."

"What are we going to do?" asked Claudia tearfully, lighting up a cigarette.

"We'll have to sell this house," replied Colette sadly.

They were identical twins, 24 years old. Both standing at 5' 5" - slim and attractive with shoulder-length blonde hair and blue eyes. Although they had their father's colouring they both had their mother's small straight nose, slightly full well-shaped lips and small, neat teeth. But the likeness ended there.

Claudia, still puffing away at her cigarette, was shy and timid. Most of the time she could be seen in sloppy sweaters, jeans and trainers, and she wore her hair loose, so that her make-up free face was usually hidden behind a golden curtain.

Colette was an air-stewardess - intelligent, confident and capable. She wore her golden hair swept up gracefully on top of her head, and her face was always beautifully made up, enhancing her lovely features. Her clothes were expensive and glamorous and she was never without a pair of high-heeled shoes. These, along with her posture, made her look much taller than her sister.

Colette put an arm round her twin's shoulders.

"We don't have to sell the house yet, Claudia, after all you still live here and I don't."

"I just don't know what to do," whined Claudia. "Oh, Colette, you're so much cleverer than me. I'm sure you've got my share of brains and confidence!"

"Don't be silly," smiled her twin. "You're a much nicer person than me - kinder and more gentle."

"I'm weak and soft, and I never know what to do."

"You just need looking after, that's all."

"I know."

They were silent for a moment, then Colette said gently, "You're thinking about Attilio, aren't you?"

"Yes. I love him so much," confided Claudia.

"Do you think he'll ask you to marry him?"

"I hope so."

Claudia worked in London in the offices of a well-known school of music. Attilio Rossini was a singing student who had done most of his training in Italy, but had come to London for one year.

"He goes back to Italy in July, doesn't he?"

"Yes."

"So if you married him, you'd probably be going to Italy to live," stated Colette.

"Yes, I would. Oh, Colette, you wouldn't mind, would you?" cried Claudia, suddenly feeling alarmed.

"No, of course not, silly. I could always come and see you when I fly over there."

"Oh, yes, that would be lovely."

"Life's a bit different over there, you know," said Colette cautiously.

"I don't care. I love Attilio."

"Well, why don't we leave the sale of the house for now. If you do marry Attilio and go to Italy, I can arrange to sell it and deposit your half of the money into you bank account. If you don't marry him, you can stay here as long as you like. I'm in no rush to sell our family home."

"Oh, Colette, you're so good to me."

"Of course I am," smiled Colette, "you're my other half! Come on, let's clean this place up."

The house was a mess, and the two women set about clearing away plates, cups, glasses and dirty ashtrays. The guests had been friends, neighbours and staff from the travel agency where their father had worked. Both their parents had been only children whose parents were dead, which left Claudia and Colette with no relations.

They tidied up and then went into the kitchen where they washed up together. By the time they had finished, it was dark outside. They drew the curtains, got themselves a bottle of wine, and sat on the settee facing the warm gas fire, quietly chatting and drinking until bedtime. Claudia smoked heavily - her cigarettes were always a comfort to her in times of stress.

The funeral had taken place on a Friday, so the two women stayed at the house for the weekend, trying to sort out their parents' affairs, and simply enjoying being together.

Early on Monday morning they went back to work - Claudia to the school of music, where she was looking forward to seeing Attilio, and Colette to the house she shared with two other air-stewardesses, so she could change into her uniform before heading for the airport.

Claudia was much too nervous to drive into London, but at the same time she hated the train journey from Borehamwood to the capital. The train was always packed and then there was the hectic tube ride from King's Cross to her destination.

Once she got off the tube she smoked a quick cigarette en route to the music school. As she walked through the doors, her heart leapt at the sight of Attilio coming towards her with swift strides. He was so handsome - a few inches taller than herself, slim with broad shoulders. His dark, shining hair was swept back from his olive-skinned face, his dark eyes lighting up beneath long, dark lashes. His sensuous mouth broke into a smile showing even, white teeth. The faint shadow of a beard touched his face.

"Claudia, my little one!" he held out his arms.

"Oh, Attilio," she cried, tears welling up in her big, blue eyes. She flew into his arms, and he hugged her tightly.

"Hey, Attilio, put her down, you don't know where she's been!" called a passing student.

Attilio looked up and grinned, then bending his head he wiped away Claudia's tears with gentle fingers.

" Meet me here at 1 o'clock - we go for lunch, yes?"

"Oh, yes!"

"I must go now, I see you later." He kissed her briefly and dashed off.

Claudia was glad to be back at work. It gave her something to do, and her colleagues were full of sympathy for the terrible and sudden loss of her parents. Still, the morning dragged.

At about 1 o'clock Claudia was standing at the main entrance of the building again when Attilio arrived. He kissed her cheek and put an arm round her shoulders.

"Come, *Cara.*" He led her away to a nearby bistro. They found a bench seat in the window and he ordered them white wine and some ham sandwiches. While they were waiting for their order Attilio turned and looked into Claudia's worried eyes.

"You are all alone now, yes?"

"Well not exactly - I do have my sister."

"But, she not live with you. She is the air-stewardess, yes?"

"Yes, that's right."

Attilio stroked her hair with a gentle hand, and smiled at her. "Then why not you marry me?"

"Marry you! Oh, Attilio!" Her face lit up.

"But of course! We can marry in July, have a few days in

Paris, and I take you home with me to Milano."

"Oh, yes, Attilio, oh, yes!" Tears of joy welled up in her eyes, and Attilio pulled her into his arms. She buried her face in his shoulder.

When their food and drink arrived, they sat eating, drinking and chatting happily about their future.

Attilio had already told Claudia about his life in Milan. His family owned shops selling expensive leather goods. His father, Flavio, was dead, and his mother Valeria lived with her widowed sister Zia Maria – Attilio's Aunt Maria. His eldest brother, Flavio jnr, lived in Rome with his wife and family, and they ran the family shop there. Another brother Sergio and his family lived in Florence, where there was another shop. The youngest brother, Bruno, was not interested in working in the shops, so he stayed at home in Milan as chauffeur and general dogsbody. Attilio also had a younger sister, Isabella, whom he adored. While Attilio had been studying music a manager had been installed in the Milan shop, and Attilio would go in and help when he was home.

Claudia was looking forward to meeting her boyfriend's family, particularly his 20-year-old sister. Claudia had visions of them making friends, going shopping and doing 'girlie' things together. She was also looking forward to living with Attilio in his huge villa and looking after him.

"I teach you to speak Italian, yes?"

"I don't think I shall be very good at that, I'm not very clever."

"You will be O.K. - my family, they will help you."

"Oh, Attilio, I can't wait! I'm so happy!"

"I make you very happy, and we will make babies together, yes?" Claudia blushed. The thought of sleeping with this wonderful man and having his children made her insides turn over. Attilio had always behaved like a gentleman towards her, which made her long for him desperately. He had very firm ideas, and although he'd had many affairs during his life, he wanted Claudia to be special. It made her love him all the more.

During the next few months Claudia and Attilio made the arrangements for their wedding. Colette would spend her free weekends helping her sister choose her wedding outfit and new clothes, and they passed many happy hours together. The wedding was to take place at the local registry office and Colette was to be bridesmaid. A few friends would attend the ceremony and then they would go on to a hotel for a small private reception. Claudia was surprised when Attilio told her that his family would not be coming to the wedding but, sensing his disappointment, she said very little.

At the end of the summer term the students performed a concert for family and friends. It was the first time Claudia had seen Attilio on stage. She was overwhelmed with pride and joy at his talent - she had never realised until then that he had such a wonderful voice. As she listened, her love for him overflowed.

The wedding day arrived - a glorious, sunny July morning. Claudia was shaking with nerves and excitement, but her twin, as usual, was cool, calm and collected.

"How do I look, Colette?"

"Absolutely gorgeous. Now stop worrying!" laughed her sister, who looked elegant in a long blue dress with blue flowers sprinkling her upswept hair.

Claudia kept checking her appearance in the mirror - she hardly recognised herself. Her golden hair was swept up on top of her head, like her sister's, in soft curls. Her head was encircled with a crown of white roses and strands of pearls hung down to her shoulders. She wore a long silky, white dress with a short-sleeved lace coat which floated to the floor. A string of pearls caressed her neck, she wore white pearly shoes on her dainty feet, and carried a bouquet of sweet-smelling pink roses.

Claudia was being given away by her boss from the school of music, who had been very kind to her after the death of her parents. Her heart ached for her dear father, who she would so have loved to be at her side.

She arrived at the Register Office looking radiant, and the sight of Attilio gazing at her with adoring eyes made her almost faint with happiness.

The service was short and deeply touching. Colette was pleased to see the love and joy between Claudia and Attilio, and prayed that her timid sister would be able to cope with a new family who had not even come to her wedding.

After the service photos were taken beneath tall, leafy trees, and then they all went to a nearby hotel for a small reception, where they enjoyed a delicious meal and drank champagne.

Early in the evening Claudia and her new husband kissed everyone goodbye before going to Gatwick Airport for their flight to Paris.

The week they spent in Paris was the happiest time of Claudia's life. She was so much in love with her husband, who was kind and a loving, gentle and experienced lover. They stayed at the Hilton Hotel in the Honeymoon Suite. They spent their days sight-seeing, visiting the Eiffel Tower, Notre Dame and the famous art galleries, where Claudia was able to see the portrait of the Mona Lisa for the first time. They spent their evenings having romantic meals in expensive restaurants, nights clubs and on a boat sailing down the Seine. One day Attilio took her shopping and bought her gifts and beautiful clothes.

Claudia enjoyed this marvellous, busy city, but was terrified of crossing the roads. The cars raced along the streets, ignoring pedestrian crossings and traffic lights, and parking anywhere they could find a space. Almost every car she saw had a bump in it!

By the end of the week they were ready to fly to Milan. Claudia was looking forward to seeing her husband's villa and meeting his family. She was happy and excited at starting her new life with Attilio.

She had no idea that her bubble of happiness was about to burst.

They arrived at Malpensa airport early on Saturday afternoon. No-one was there to meet them so they got a taxi to Attilio's home.

Soon they drew up outside the Villa Carlotta. As they got out of the taxi, Attilio collected their luggage and Claudia stared up at her beautiful new home, which was bathed in sunshine. It was a large, white building with a terracotta tiled roof. Its many windows boasted window boxes spilling over with colourful flowers. There were stone steps leading up to a large wooden door, and the garden was lawned with flower beds, fountains and statues.

"Oh, Attilio, it's beautiful!" she breathed.

"A beautiful house for a beautiful lady," he replied, smiling.

The taxi driver helped Attilio with their luggage, and the three of them made their way to the front door. Attilio unlocked it and they walked in. Attilio paid the driver and he left.

Claudia found herself standing in a large hall with a light, marble floor, surrounded by wooden doors, large vases of flowers and statues.

The house was silent.

Attilio suddenly called out, "Mama, Zia Maria, Bruno, Isabella......come and meet my bride!"

Doors slowly opened and Claudia's heart sank as she found herself looking into a sea of hostile faces.

Attilio introduced Claudia to his family.

"Cara, meet Mama." Claudia stared at her mother-in-law - Valeria Rossini. She was short and plump. Her dark hair, streaked with grey, was scraped back into a bun at the nape of her neck. Her dark, piercing eyes and beaky nose made her look like an eagle. Her mouth was tight and unfriendly. She nodded to Claudia.

"H - hello" stammered Claudia."

"My aunt ...Zia Maria."

Claudia stared at his aunt, who looked like the mother, only taller and fatter. Zia Maria also nodded curtly.

Claudia was getting more nervous by the minute, and her legs were beginning to tremble.

She was then introduced to her brother-in-law, Bruno. He looked like Attilio, but was a little taller and much stockier - his shoulders were broader, his arms and legs fatter. He stared at Claudia without speaking, his hands tucked into the pockets of his jeans, his black T-shirt hanging loosely over his big hips.

Attilio put an arm round Claudia's shaking shoulders.

"Cara, this is my little sister, Isabella," he smiled, proudly.

"Hello," stammered Claudia, her heart thumping, as she gazed at her sister-in-law. Isabella was the same height as Claudia, and slim with long dark hair, which she tossed over her shoulder. Large dark unfriendly eyes stared at Claudia under long, dark lashes. Isabella had a rather long nose and a sulky mouth, but she looked attractive in a tight-fitting white designer T-shirt and blue jeans.

Suddenly they were all chatting away in Italian, and Claudia felt lost, lonely and afraid. They all ignored her. After a few minutes Attilio took her arm and guided her towards a large staircase.

"Come, Cara. I show you to our rooms."

Feeling rather bewildered, she mounted the staircase, Bruno following with their luggage.

They climbed the stairs, reached the top, then went up a few more steps which led to a long corridor.

"These are our rooms," smiled Attilio as he led her through a door on the right and proceeded to show her round, each room leading through to the next by large, carved wooden doors. The door on the right led to the living room, with a small kitchen leading off the side, which looked out over a large and beautiful back garden. A door at the far end of the living room led into a big bedroom that stretched across the width of the villa, one window looking over the back garden and the other looking out over the front. A door at this end led to a spacious, tiled bathroom. All the floors were of polished wood, the ceilings high and ornate. The walls were white and covered in pictures of flowers and birds and scenery. The furniture was of heavy, carved oak and the settee and armchairs were covered with plush, flowered fabric.

While Claudia was being shown round her quarters Bruno had brought up the rest of their luggage. She stared at his retreating back and frowned.

"What is wrong, Cara?" asked Attilio placing his hands on her shoulders.

"D.....do..all your family live here too?"

"But of course!"

"I.....I thought we would be on our own!"

"But there is much room here, and I look after my family now my father is dead."

"But what if *we* have a family?"

"There will be enough room for us all, do not worry."

"Your family don't like me."

"Don't be silly, Cara. You are a stranger now, but soon they will love you as I do."

Claudia sighed and turning away, she picked up her bag, fished out her cigarettes and lighter and lit up. She breathed in the smoke nervously. Attilio went and fetched her an ashtray.

"Sit down, Cara. I get us some wine, yes?"

"Oh, yes please."

Attilio went into the kitchen, which was small but well-fitted with cupboards, cooker, washing machine and fridge. He returned to the living room with a bottle of white wine and two glasses. They sat on the settee together and held hands. He smiled down at Claudia, his eyes warm.

"We look after ourselves here, but we have our evening meal with my family. When we finish this wine we unpack and then I take you out, yes?"

"Yes, that'll be nice," Claudia replied, trying to sound cheerful when her heart was heavy.

After unpacking their clothes, they set off by car to the local supermarket, where they bought a supply of cigarettes for Claudia and some food - bread, milk, eggs, butter, sugar, coffee, wine and some fresh fruit and salad.

When they returned to the villa, they put away the shopping and went for a walk round the extensive grounds of the villa. They wandered through trees and lawns and beds of flowers, and Claudia admired the swimming pool, the statues and fountains. Attilio introduced her to the gardener, who was clearing the garden after his siesta.

At 7.30 they went back to their rooms to shower and change for dinner.

"We have missed our siesta - we have the early night, yes?" grinned Attilio. Claudia blushed.

Claudia suffered the evening meal in silence. They all sat round a large table in the huge dining room on the ground floor. Staff, dressed formally in black and white, served at the table. The family chatted to Attilio but totally ignored Claudia. She picked at her food nervously, hardly noticing what she was eating. Her sad face was hidden between curtains of hair.

Claudia sat between Attilio and Bruno, and was more than thankful when Bruno lit up a cigarette after their meal. She lit one gratefully and he shared the ashtray with her.

Her mother-in-law glared at her with disgust, but Claudia bravely ignored her.

Later that night she lay in bed staring unhappily at the ceiling. Attilio breathed deeply beside her, his face nestled into her neck, his right arm lying heavily across her waist. Tears of misery rolled down her face and onto her neck.

"What have I done?" she thought miserably. "What have I done? His family hate me, and I hate them. I always will, and yet I've got to live here with them."

Claudia tried to think of horrible names for them all. His mother she would have to call the "old witch" and the awful Zia Maria... she could call her Zia Nastya, because she was so nasty. She thought about big, horrible Bruno... she would call him "the Bulk" - that suited him perfectly. And as for pouty Isabella... she would call her "the Sulk". Claudia smiled sadly to herself in the darkness..the "Bulk" and the "Sulk" - what a pair!

Feeling a little better she turned her head and laid her cheek against her husband's soft, dark hair.

She eventually drifted off into an uneasy sleep.

TWO

A NEW LIFE 1970-2

Attilio Rossini adored his wife and was worried when he saw her unhappy face the following morning.

"What is wrong, Cara?"

"Oh, Attilio, I was so happy and excited when I knew I was coming to Italy with you, but now I am here it all seems so strange. And your family - I know they don't like me."

"That is not so, Cara, they say you are very beautiful."

"But they don't speak to me."

Attilio smiled. "This is because you not speak Italian. Mama and Maria, they speak no English, and Bruno and Isabella speak only a little. Tomorrow is Monday - we go into Milano centre and I show you round, and I get you a book to help you to speak our language. O.K?"

She nodded.

"Today, Cara, my other brothers and their families, they come to meet you and we have a big party."

"That will be nice," she replied, hoping that the rest of the family were going to be more friendly.

"Claudia, why not you phone your sister? The phone it is here - my private line," he chuckled.

"Oh, yes, I'd love to," she smiled.

Attilio found the codes for her to ring England, and while she was ringing Colette, he went downstairs to speak to his family.

"Colette, it's Claudia."

"Hi there, how are you?"

"I'm fine."

"How was Paris?"

"Marvellous!"

"And how's Italy?"

"Attilio's home is beautiful- it's a great big villa set in lovely grounds - it's on the outskirts of Milan."

"That's great! And what are his family like?"

"Awful!"

"Awful - why?"

"His mother and aunt are like something out of the ark! They wear drab old-fashioned clothes and their hair is scraped back in a bun, and they look like two old crows. His brother, Bruno, is big and fat and not very bright, and his sister is pretty but sulks all the time. To make matters worse they don't speak English, so they don't talk to me. And, worse still, they all live here!"

"Live there? Can't you persuade Attilio to get a place of your own?"

"He can't, the villa belongs to him now and he promised his father he would look after them. I don't think they like me, Colette."

"Give them time, Sis, they'll probably be alright."

"Yes, maybe. I'm going to have to learn Italian, that'll probably help."

"I'm sure it will. I'll try and get over to see you soon."

"Oh, please do - I'd love to see you."

They chatted on for a while.

By late morning, Attilio's other two other brothers and their families had arrived. Claudia had dressed in a pretty blue and white striped summer dress and white high-heeled sandals, her shining golden hair falling softly round her face.

"You look so beautiful, Cara," Attilio had whispered to her as they made their way downstairs.

Claudia was first introduced to her eldest brother-in-law, Flavio, who was small, neat and dark, and his wife Paula, who was short, dark and chubby. They greeted her warmly and kissed her cheeks. Their young son, Lorenzo, and daughter, Zeta, were scampering about, getting in everyone's way.

Next to be introduced was Sergio, who was also small and dark, but rather solemn. He had black hair which curled round his acquiline face. His wife, Anna, was small, thin and rather plain, with her black hair cut very short. They both greeted Claudia politely as their little son, Mario, jumped up and down excitedly, his black curls bobbing.

After introductions were made everyone made their way outside. It was a beautiful hot day, and a long table had been set on the patio. Bruno was happily cooking meat on a barbecue, while the cook/housekeeper and her daughter, filled the table with mounds of food and bottles of wine.

Eventually they all settled down and the rest of the day was spent eating, drinking and talking round the table. The only person who really talked to Claudia was Flavio's wife, Paula, who spoke some English.

Claudia sat and picked at her food miserably. She hated pasta, and found the food too oily, with too much tomato sauce. But she ate a bit of salad and meat, and drank plenty of wine.

The day dragged on and by evening Claudia had had enough. She got up and left the table with a glass of wine and her cigarettes, and went and sat on a wooded seat surrounded by shrubs and trees near a large fountain. She sat and watched the cascading water sparkling in the late afternoon sun.

She looked up and smiled as she saw Paula approach.

"Hello, Claudia, are they giving you a bad time?" Paula said as she sat down beside her new sister-in-law.

"I'm afraid so. I know they don't like me."

"Do you know why?"

"No."

"I will tell you. The family, they wanted Attilio to marry the daughter of one of their friends. She is also the best friend of Isabella."

"Oh, no!" gasped Claudia.

"I am afraid so, but do not worry - they did not like me at first, but now they are alright. Once our first child was born I was suddenly one of the family."

The two of them chatted for a while until Attilio came and dragged them back to the house.

Claudia liked Paula, and was disappointed that she lived in Rome not Milan.

The following day, as promised, Attilio took Claudia into the centre of Milan. It was a beautiful city full of historic buildings, churches and museums. There were streets brimming with wonderful shops and trams trundling along the roads. The Metro reminded Claudia of London, though it had a more romantic name than the Underground.

Attilio proudly showed her the famous La Scala Opera House, where he hoped to sing one day. He then took her to the Rossini family leather shop to meet the staff, who were very polite and showed her round. Her eyes lit up at the sight of the beautiful leather clothes, shoes and bags. Attilio gave her a matching handbag and shoes in soft cream leather, his eyes lighting up at the pleasure in her face.

Next he bought Claudia a book to help her learn Italian, and then they spent a couple of hours sitting in the sun outside a cafe, eating, drinking and watching the world go by.

Claudia's spirits sank as she got back to the Villa Carlotta, and was met in the hall by Zia Nastya, who gave her a filthy look when she spotted the shopping bags Claudia was carrying.

While Attilio was waiting for his agent to contact him for work, he took Claudia on many days out to show her his country, which was truly beautiful with its mountains, lakes and waterfalls. Claudia was enthralled with the old castles, churches and cathedrals and the villas with white walls and red roofs, snuggling amongst the trees. She loved the large towns with their museums and art galleries and statues, and the little houses perched on the edge of rivers. They spent a weekend at the lovely Lake Como, and Claudia almost wept with relief at being away from her husband's family.

After a couple of weeks Attilio got a phone call from his agent, who had got him a job singing in a high-class night club in Milan, three nights a week. He started rehearsals with a backing group, and Claudia suddenly found herself alone during the day. Attilio told her that if she wanted to go out anywhere, Bruno would take her in the car. Claudia hated Bruno and felt uncomfortable in his presence, but sometimes she did need to go out and get food and cigarettes. She looked after herself during the day, and never joined the family for the evening meal. No-one ever came to her rooms to find her.

She spent most of her time in their rooms, phoning her sister, cleaning and tidying up, and making the place as homely as possible. She tried to learn Italian with the help of her book, but found it very difficult. She wasn't sure how to pronounce most of the words, and was totally confused to find that some words were masculine, ending in an 'o', and some were feminine and ending in an 'a'. Putting words into a sentence was a nightmare, as the words were all spoken in a different order. Claudia was totally baffled, although she did manage to learn a few words such as *si* for yes, *no* for no, *per favore* for please and *grazie* for thank you. Some of the words were simple such as *madre* for mother, *padre* for father, *sorella* for sister and *fratello* for brother.

Once Attilio started singing in the evenings, she was on her own even more. He spent his days rehearsing new songs, and after his late nights, would sleep late in the mornings. Claudia was getting more and more lonely and her in-laws more hostile. If she ever tried to complain about them, Attilio would not listen… he was more interested in getting her into bed.

One weekend, Valeria's family came to visit – they were from Sicily. Claudia didn't like them on sight, they looked conceited and sly. She hoped they weren't Mafia – they certainly looked just as she had always imagined such people would look. She caught Bruno's sly grin of satisfaction when her face paled with alarm as she was introduced to them. Claudia simply scuttled back up to her rooms and kept out of their way.

When their visitors were gone, Valeria, Maria and Bruno sat talking about Claudia.

"Why did my son have to marry that stupid English girl? She is just a money-grabbing tart!"

"She won't last long here," snapped Maria. "She is weak and spineless and as scared as a rabbit!"

"We'll make sure she doesn't - the sooner she gets out of here, the better, and then Attilio can marry a good Catholic, Italian girl." Bruno started to laugh. "Did you see her face when we told her your family were from Sicily, Mama? I am sure she thinks we are Mafia. She was so frightened!"

"Well, let her think it," retorted Valeria nastily.

The weeks flew by. Summer dwindled into autumn and autumn into winter, and the weather grew cold. Claudia was desperately unhappy and lonely and began to lose weight. She filled her days cleaning their rooms, preparing herself light meals, smoking and drinking and gazing out of the window. She would sometimes put on the T.V. to try and learn some Italian, but everyone spoke too fast.

Colette managed a couple of visits, bringing her some books to read and some jigsaws and duty-free cigarettes. The two of them would go shopping together, have meals out, and talk for hours.

"I see what you mean about your in-laws, Sis, they are awful, so nasty and miserable. They're like something out of a horror film." Colette had giggled.

The feeling was mutual between the Rossinis and Colette. They hated Claudia's timidness, they hated Colette's glamour and confidence even more.

When Attilio was home, Claudia always tried to be cheerful. She did not want him to worry about her and she made no further comments about his family as she knew he loved them.

One day he came in full of excitement.

"Claudia. I have wonderful news. I have a part in an opera!"

"Oh, that's marvellous, when do you start?"

"We start rehearsals in December, and the show, it start in January."

"Where?"

"Rome."

"Rome?"

"Si, I will stay with Flavio and come home to you at weekends." Claudia was devastated, but remained silent.

Attilio was a great fan of the late Mario Lanza, and had always wanted to be like him. Now his chance had come, and he was walking on air.

On Attilio's last night at the night club, he took Claudia with him. She was enthralled at his wonderful performance, but it wasn't until she joined the party after the show that she realised just how popular he was, especially with women.

The following day Claudia was very quiet.

"What is wrong, Cara?"

"I shall miss you so much, Attilio."

He smiled. "How you like to come to Rome with me? You can go the Christmas shopping with Paula..." Claudia flung her arms round his neck.

"Oh, Attilio, oh yes, oh yes!" Her husband laughed and hugged her, glad to see her looking so happy. She spent the afternoon sorting out their clothes and packing suitcases, while Attilio sang to her.

When Attilio came home, the whole villa seemed to come alive. He was always so full of life and energy, singing and laughing and dashing about. When he was gone, the place seemed to die.

Claudia spent a wonderful three weeks in Rome, even though the weather was bitterly cold. During the days she would either play with Lorenzo and Zeta or go shopping or sightseeing with Paula, leaving the children with the au pair.

One day Paula took her to their shop in the centre of Rome. Attilio had told Claudia to take whatever she wanted from the shop for Christmas. She chose a beautiful, three-quarter length brown leather coat with a fur-trimmed hood, and a matching pair of boots and large handbag. In the meantime, Attilio bought her an expensive gold bracelet as a surprise for Christmas Day.

In the evenings they would all sit round the table, eating drinking and chatting as usual, and listening to Attilio tell them about the rehearsals for the opera and the costumes he would be wearing. Some evenings they would go out for a meal or go to a night-club, where Claudia and Attilio would dance together under the spotlights and he would softly sing love songs in her ear.

As Christmas drew near Claudia, Attilio and Flavio and his family all drove to Milan.

"Back to the prison!" thought Claudia, as they drove through snow and ice back to the villa which now sparkled in the winter sunshine.

The Villa Carlotta was a hive of activity over Christmas, with so many people staying in it. On Christmas Day they all exchanged presents. Claudia received perfume and chocolates from Valeria, Maria and Isabella. When she opened her gift from Bruno, she was mortified to find an English/Italian dictionary. Bruno sneered at her discomfort.

Claudia was sorry to see Flavio and his family leave after Christmas, especially Paula. What would happen at New Year? She was soon to find out.

"Claudia, I take you away for New Year," Attilio announced one day.

"Where are we going?"

"It is a surprise!"

Claudia packed suitcases with growing excitement, and the following morning Bruno took them to the airport.

"New Year, I go ski-ing, but after the death of your parents, I not take you to the mountains."

Her eyes filled with tears. "Thank you, Attilio. I'm so grateful."

He smiled down at her lovingly.

They arrived at the airport and checked in. When Claudia realised that they were flying to Gatwick, she squealed with excitement.

"We're going to London to see Colette!" she cried.

Attilio laughed. "You like my surprise?"

"Oh, yes, you really are wonderful!"

They spent a few marvellous days in London. Colette had arranged for them to stay in a hotel as there was not enough room at her house, which she shared with two other girls. Claudia was able to look up old friends and introduce her handsome husband, and on New Year's Eve, Colette took them to a fabulous party.

Claudia felt truly happy and her sister was relieved to see her and Attilio still very much in love.

During the afternoon before their return to Italy, the two sisters were chatting together.

"You're looking well, Claudia."

"I'm fine when I'm with Attilio," she smiled at her sister. "Keep a secret?"

"Of course."

"I think I'm pregnant," whispered Claudia.

"You're not sure?"

"Well, I'm two weeks late."

"Have you told Attilio?"

"Not yet. I want to surprise him."

"Won't he notice you're late?"

"No, I don't think so, he gets so excited about things, he doesn't always think."

"Well, congratulations, Sis. I'm dying to be an auntie!"

Claudia didn't keep her secret from Attilio for long. The morning after her return to Italy, she rose to get out of bed, and as she made her way to the bathroom, she felt sick and faint, her body broke out in a cold sweat, and her face turned as white as a sheet.

"What is wrong, my little one?" called Attilio.

"I feel sick." She staggered to the bathroom, fell to her knees and vomited into the toilet. Attilio rushed into the bathroom.

"Cara, what is wrong?" he asked urgently.

She smiled at him weakly. "I think I am pregnant."

"Pregnant?"

"Having a baby," she explained.

"A baby, but this is wonderful!"

Claudia rinsed out her mouth with cold water, and Attilio picked her up in his arms and carried back to bed. She felt sick and faint all morning, although she was a little better by the afternoon, and rested on the settee.

Claudia felt the same every day, and when Attilio had to leave for Rome, he left her behind.

"You must stay here, Cara, my family will look after you."

"Like hell they will," she thought bitterly.

"I return after the show on Saturday nights and I stay until Mondays. I telephone you while I am away."

Claudia was devastated, as she had hoped to go to Rome with Attilio. But she knew she would be a burden to him if she was sick all the time.

When Attilio finally left for Rome, she lay on their bed and wept.

THREE

FEAR AND JOY 1972-3

The next three months passed in a haze. Claudia felt so ill during the mornings and tired in the afternoons. Her thin body grew rapidly and her skirts and jeans soon became too tight. Although her in-laws knew about the baby, they still ignored her and no-one ever came up to her rooms to see how she was.

"I could be lying here dying or having a miscarriage and nobody would know or care, " she thought, miserably. She hardly ever went out; only when she was desperate for some shopping or cigarettes did she ask Bruno to take her to the supermarket. Although Attilio always left her plenty of money she still would not go out and catch a bus or get a taxi, as she still could not speak the language. She grew more lonely and unhappy.

By the time she was three months pregnant, Attilio had arranged for her to see the family doctor, and Bruno took her for her first appointment. He waited for her outside.

When she saw the doctor, he weighed her and took her blood pressure, and then she lay on the couch for him to examine her. Suddenly he frowned and picked up his stethoscope. He placed it slowly on parts of her abdomen, then looked up and smiled at her.

"*Signora Rossini - gemelli.*"

"*Gemelli?*" she frowned.

"*Si, Signora*, twins."

"Twins, oh, my goodness!" she cried.

"In your family - you have the twins, yes?"

"Yes. I am a twin. We are identical."

"Then perhaps they will also be."

Claudia was thrilled.

The doctor gave her a date at the beginning of September, but told her to be prepared to have her twins at least one month early.

When Claudia got back to the car she said nothing to Bruno. She wanted Attilio to be the first to hear her exciting news.

While she was waiting for him to call she sat thinking how wonderful it would be to have two babies. She would be able to spend her lonely days looking after them. It wouldn't matter any more that her in-laws ignored her; she would have her two children to keep her company, and as they grew she would be able to play with them and talk to them. They would be such good company.

Attilio finally rang before he left for the theatre. When she told him, he was thrilled.

"Cara, this is wonderful - you are a clever girl to give me two babies," he laughed. "Have you told Mama?"

"Er... no. I wasn't sure she would understand me, and I wanted you to know first."

"Is O.K., my little one. I will ring her."

The Rossinis were delighted to hear the news. They loved children, and were looking forward to having two new babies arriving in the family. They made their plans about bringing them up, but said nothing to Claudia.

When Attilio got home during the early hours of Sunday morning, Claudia was still awake. As he got into bed he gave her a big hug, and they chatted happily together.

"What shall we call them?" she asked.

"If we have two boys, I think we call them Attilio jnr. and Claudio, after us. What you think?"

"I think that's a lovely idea!"

"And what if we have two girls?"

"I'd like one of them to be called Lucy, after my mother."

"O.K. and we call the other one Valeria after my mother." Claudia reluctantly agreed.

"What if we have one of each?"

"Lucy and Attilio jnr?" she suggested.

"Yes, I like that."

They talked for a long time before falling asleep.

Now the first three months were over Claudia was feeling better in the mornings, but Attilio wanted her to remain in Milan, in case anything went wrong, she would be better off at home.

As Attilio was away all week, he suggested that Claudia should invite her sister over for a week, and she could help Claudia choose items for the twins and order anything she wanted.

Claudia wasted no time phoning her sister.

"Hi, Colette."

"Hi there, Sis, how you doing?"

"Colette, you know you mentioned how much weight I'd put on in such a short time?"

"Yes."

"Well, I'm having twins."

"Oh, that's wonderful, Sis. In fact I did wonder whether you might be, but I didn't mention it because I didn't want to worry you."

"I'm so thrilled, Colette. Now can you come over for a week?"

"Course I can. I'll get some holiday fixed up, and when you've had the twins I'll come over for a couple of weeks and give you a hand."

"That would be great!"

Colette came to Milan a fortnight later, and Bruno took Claudia to the airport to meet her. As usual the two sisters hugged each other affectionately.

"My, aren't you getting tubby!" laughed Colette.

"I know, I can't believe how big I've got."

The two of them spent an enjoyable week together - going

into Milan most days to buy maternity clothes for Claudia for when she grew even larger. They were mainly summer dresses as she would be at her largest during the hot summer months. They bought a few items for the babies such as little vests, babygrows, bibs and disposable nappies. Claudia would not normally have bought so much at this stage, but she wanted to shop with her sister and this was an ideal opportunity. They chose and ordered a large double pram, two cots and two cradles which would be paid for and delivered nearer the time. They also looked round at bottles and sterilisers and tiny car seats and baby baths, which they would buy later.

Each day they went in to Milan. They would shop in the morning, stopping at noon for a light lunch, then return to the Villa Carlotta for Claudia to rest, as she seemed permanently tired. In the evenings they would either go out for a meal, or Colette would cook at home and they would sit chatting.

On the Saturday before Colette's return, Bruno drove them to Rome, where the two sisters went to see Attilio in his opera.

"My God," whispered Colette, "he's fantastic!"

"I know, he's wonderful, isn't he?"

"It won't be long before he's famous, you know, Sis."

"That's what's worrying me. If he does become famous I'll hardly ever see him at all."

"You'll have the twins, won't you!"

"I know, but I still worry that I won't see much of Attilio."

"Don't be such a pessimist!" laughed Colette.

After Colette had gone Claudia felt desolate. The weeks flew by and she grew huge, uncomfortable and depressed. She began to drink and smoke heavily to calm her nerves, even though she knew it was wrong. Colette paid another visit during the summer and helped Claudia finish buying all the things she needed for the twins.

Everything had been arranged for the birth. A nursery was decorated and furnished and Claudia had been booked into a private nursing home, the "Gardenia", to have her babies, which had its own premature baby unit, as the twins would most likely be born early. Attilio had also arranged to take two weeks holiday to be with his wife, his understudy taking his place.

In June it was Claudia's birthday. She was six months pregnant. For her birthday, Attilio bought her a very expensive gold necklace - a heavy gold chain with a golden "Gemini" which hung down on her chest.

"Gemini for the twins, yes?" Attilio had smiled.

"It's simply beautiful. I shall wear it for ever!" she had cried.

By the seventh month of her pregnancy, Claudia was so big she could hardly move. She spent most of her lonely days sitting on the settee with a hand on her swollen body, feeling her babies wriggling and kicking about.

On the Saturday night, hours before Attilio was due home, she was lying in bed when her waters broke. She lay still in bed, terrified to move in case she gave birth all on her own. When Attilio finally got home, he found her frightened and in tears.

"Why you not fetch Mama, my little one?"

"I was too scared to get out of bed," she wept. Attilio put his arms round her.

"Do not worry, my little one, I will take you to the hospital." He left the room and ran downstairs to wake Isabella. He shouted to her to get a bag for Claudia, with nightdresses and toiletries. He woke Bruno and told him to get the car ready, then ran back into the bedroom to pick up his terrified wife. He took her in his arms and carried her down to the car. Bruno put his foot down and they sped to the "Gardenia", where, after Attilio's frantic phone call, the staff were waiting.

Claudia was so relieved to get to the hospital, where the nurses fussed round her. She was examined and put to bed, then given an injection, as the nursing staff were concerned about the babies' lungs. Attilio sat with her all night, and the following morning she gave birth to identical twin boys, who were rushed away to be put into incubators.

After she had been stitched, washed and changed, and given a light breakfast, Claudia and Attilio were allowed to see their tiny sons, Attilio jnr. and Claudio, who weighed in at just over four pounds. Claudia was helped into a wheelchair and Attilio pushed her along to the baby unit to see their newborn sons lying in their incubators. Wires from their tiny bodies were attached to monitors and 'drips' attached to each little hand.

"Oh, look!" gasped Claudia. "Aren't they beautiful!"

"They are so tiny," whispered Attilio.

"They have your black hair, and they look like you," she murmured happily.

"Let us hope they are as sweet as you," murmured Attilio, squeezing her shoulders from behind.

Eventually Claudia was taken up to a private room. She was told that the twins would have to remain in the hospital until they had put on weight and were feeding properly, but Claudia would be allowed to stay with them.

While Claudia was resting, Attilio rang his family and Colette with the news. He and Colette agreed to take their holidays as soon as Claudia and the twins arrived home.

Claudia spent a happy three weeks in the hospital, feeding, changing and bathing her two tiny sons, whom she now called Tilly and Claudy. Her lovely face was filled with joy as she nursed and cuddled them. Attilio visited at weekends, and Colette made a flying visit with flowers and little blue outfits for her two nephews.

"Claudia, they're absolutely gorgeous, and don't they look like Attilio! Let's hope they grow up as handsome."

Claudia's in-laws made a couple of visits, and although Valeria drooled over her little grandsons, she never spoke to Claudia.

After three weeks, mother and babies were allowed home. Attilio collected his family and proudly drove them back to the Villa Carlotta.

"The nursery is all ready, my little one."

"Are the cradles in our room?" she asked hopefully.

"Oh, no, Cara. The twins will go straight into the nursery."

"But I have to feed them during the night!"

"There is no need, Mama, Maria and Isabella will do this. You can rest and get back your strength."

Claudia swallowed her disappointment. She didn't want his beastly family looking after her babies, but she did not want to upset Attilio by complaining.

"Can't I have a nanny to help me?" she asked nervously. Attilio laughed.

"There is no need,Cara, when there are three women in the house to help you, and they are family."

Claudia was not happy with her husband's decision and his obsession with 'family'. She was still wondering if his family were a part of the Mafia - the thought terrified her.

The next two weeks were happy but hectic. Colette arrived as promised and she helped Claudia and Attilio look after the twins. The days were a whirl of non-stop feeding, changing, bathing and nursing the two demanding infants. It didn't take Claudia long to realise that she could not possibly manage them both on her own, especially when they were both crying lustily at the same time.

The twins' nursery, which was on the first landing, was fully equipped with cupboards, drawers, sink, washing machine and a bathroom.

Once Colette and Attilio had gone, his family took over. Every time Claudia went to the nursery, her little sons had been fed, changed and were asleep, and she was literally pushed out. The "old witch" or "Zia Nastya" were always in there, usually with Isabella. They would glare at Claudia whenever she walked in. They frightened her so much she would scuttle back to her room crying. She ended up being more lonely and miserable than she was before they were born. Although they did not speak to her it was easy enough to understand the words "stupida" (stupid), and "inglese" (Englishwoman) and "silenzio" (shut up), and she soon learned that "vai via" meant "go away".

Claudia was so depressed when Attilio was away. She adored her little sons and couldn't bear to see them being looked after by his family when she wanted to do it herself. The only time she ever managed to cuddle one of them was when Isabella was "on duty". She would glare sulkily at Claudia, but never tried to stop her. By the nervous look in Isabella's eyes Claudia realised that Isabella was as scared of her family as Claudia was herself.

The only time Claudia was able to look after her sons was when Attilio was home. He would enter the villa like a whirlwind and simply take over. As always, he was full of life and energy. He adored his little sons and he and Claudia did everything for them, and took them for walks in their big pram. By the time they were crawling, in different directions, Claudia found that she and Attilio were worn out!

During this time, the twins were christened. It hadn't occurred to Claudia that the family were Roman Catholic and she wasn't. The christening took place in a beautiful, old church. Colette and Isabella were the two godmothers, and Flavio, Sergio, Bruno and Attilio's agent and good friend were the godfathers. After the christening there was a huge party at the villa and many photographs were taken. Claudia's favourites were the ones of herself and Attilio with the boys, and another of herself with her sister, holding one twin each.

By the time the twins had passed their first birthday they had started to say their first words - in Italian! Claudia was upset - but when she approached Attilio he simply told her that she lived in Italy and it was up to her to learn the language. She did try by reading her book and leaving the T.V. on so that her ears could get used to the flow of the language. She attempted to memorisse vocabulary and learn how to pronounce the words properly, but it was hard as there was no-one to help her.

Sometimes she felt that her little sons didn't know she was their mother - they saw more of her in-laws than they did of her. She grew angry and frustrated.

By September Claudia was almost at the end of her tether, and when Attilio came home one weekend and told her that the opera was going on tour, she burst into tears.

"How long will you be gone and where?" she cried.

"We travel round Europe until Christmas. We come home for two weeks and then we go to Australia for six weeks."

Claudia was horrified "Oh, Attilio. No. no!"

"I am sorry, Cara, but to sing - it is in my blood- it is my life."

"I know, but can't I come with you? I don't want to be left here."

"Of course you can, Cara, but the babies - they stay here."

"But I couldn't leave them!" she wailed.

"Then you stay here, my little one."

Claudia was grief-stricken and angry when Attilio had gone and her in-laws got worse and made her life a misery. They kept her away from her sons as much as they could. They called her horrible names and insulted her.

One day Bruno had taken her shopping, and as he dropped her bags on the kitchen floor he spoke to her.

"You lonely without Attilio?"

"What... what do you mean?" she stammered.

"You want man?"

"Certainly not!" she snapped.

"Attilio... he get lonely... he like women..."

"Get out!" she cried angrily. "Get out!"

Bruno grinned and sauntered off.

Claudia slammed the door shut after him, and leaned against it. She was shocked to the core. Surely Attilio was not being unfaithful to her? It didn't bear thinking about.

"No. no!" she cried to herself. "Please, no! I couldn't bear it if he was sleeping with other women. I could never forgive him!" But although Claudia didn't think that Attilio would cheat on her - the seeds of doubt had been sown.

Leaving the shopping on the floor, she went to the fridge, and got out a bottle of wine and a glass and wandered thoughtfully into the lounge. With shaking fingers she lit a cigarette.

"Bruno," she thought,"is a big, fat pig. I hate him!" With tears in her eyes, she picked up her glass and downed half of her wine in one swig. She sat there, cloaked in misery. Suddenly the phone rang. She dashed over to it and picked up the receiver. It was Colette.

"Hi, Sis, how are you?"

"Oh, Colette, I'm so glad you've phoned!"

"I had a feeling something was wrong, love, what is it?"

Claudia told her about Bruno's cruel remarks.

"Bruno's wrong, Claudia. I'm sure Attilio wouldn't cheat on you, he loves you very much."

"I know, but he's away a lot, and he's with all those beautiful women, he might be tempted. I'm so unhappy, Colette."

"Look Sis, I'm off in a couple of days, I'll come over."

"I wish you were here now, I'm so lonely and fed up."

"Don't worry, I'll be with you soon."

Claudia was overjoyed to see her sister. Colette was totally unafraid of the Rossini family, and would march into the nursery to see her nephews, totally ignoring the "watchdogs".

On the afternoon of her arrival the two sisters walked into the nursery to find Isabella putting the twins into their cots for their afternoon nap. Colette looked at Isabella, pointed to the door and said.

"Out!"

Isabella glared at her, tossed her dark hair over her shoulder, and slunk out of the room.

"How do you do it?" gasped Claudia.

"It's easy for me, I don't live here. I wouldn't be so brave if I were in your shoes."

The sisters settled the boys down, and when they had gone to sleep, they sat talking quietly to each other and Claudia told Colette how unhappy she was.

"Why don't you leave here and come home with me? I could help you look after the boys."

"I've already thought of it, but it would be impossible."

"Why?"

"Well, first of all I would need help, a lot of help. Even if you helped me it wouldn't work. We would never get past the door to start with. I never get a chance to be with the twins on my own. Attilio's family would never let us out of this room, never mind the house. Then I would need the double push-chair, the cots, the high chairs and all their clothes, and that's without all my things. It would be impossible."

"Well if we could get them out, I could buy all those things and have them at my house ready for them."

"But what about the other girls in your house? There wouldn't be room."

"I only rent a room. I don't own the house. I could get us a place of our own. That reminds me. I've settled all Mum and Dad's estate, and I've put your share of the money into your bank account." She named a huge sum. Claudia gasped.

"Where did all that money come from?"

"Well, there was the sale of the house, which brought a lot. Then there was their insurance policies. The travel agency paid for the funeral and all the expense of flying Mum and Dad home. Then there were both of their cars and some shares."

"Goodness, if I came home I wouldn't have to worry about money."

"Then why don't you?" Claudia paused.

"I'm... I'm… too scared."

"Why?"

"Colette... I... I... think I've married into the Mafia."

"The Mafia! Good God, Claudia, you can't be serious!"

"It's true. The old witch's family come from Sicily, and I've heard them mention Mafia when they've been talking."

"Have you asked Attilio?"

"No. Because if it's really true, I don't want to know, and if it's not he might be angry with me."

Colette was appalled. She looked her twin straight in the eye. "Have you any idea how dangerous they are?"

"Yes, I do. That's why I'm so scared. If I took the twins, they would come after me... they would probably cut my throat, and bring the boys back here anyway."

Colette got up and started to pace the floor, rubbing an

elegant hand across her chin. She looked down at Claudia and whispered, "If you leave here, Sis, you'll have to leave on your own."

"I know."

"God, what a mess!"

"I know. I don't know which way to turn."

"I've got an idea in my mind... I'll get to work on it. If you ever decide to leave, ring me, and I'll get you out of here."

"O.K."

Suddenly Zia Nastya walked through the door.

"Get out!" snapped Colette, her eyes flashing. Maria looked at Colette, her eyes hard, and left.

"That old bag gives me the creeps," shuddered Colette.

Claudia and Colette spent the next two days looking after the twins. Colette spent the night on the settee to keep the Rossinis away. She adored her little nephews, and would kiss, cuddle and play with them with her sister, who was always relieved and happy to be with her twin. She was dreading Colette's return to England.

When Colette left for London, she gave her twin a big hug.

"Don't forget - if you want to get away, ring me."

"I promise."

Claudia was more depressed than ever after her sister's departure. She was growing thin again, and her hair was falling out in handfuls. She would weep with despair and would lie on her bed for hours, suffering terrible headaches. As usual, no-one ever came up to see her or ask if she was alright.

When Attilio phoned, she always tried to sound cheerful, not wanting to worry him. She also knew how much he loved his career and did not want to give him any problems by begging him to come home.

But as Christmas drew near, she almost dreaded him coming home. What if he had been unfaithful to her? What if had slept with a lot of women? What if he'd caught a horrible disease? Her mind was going round in circles, and her heart was aching.

When Attilio finally got home, he greeted his family, hugged his two little sons, then dashed up the stairs to his wife. He burst through the door, calling her name. Claudia took one look at the love and longing in his face, and ran to him.

"Attilio!" she cried.

"Claudia, Cara, I have missed you so!"

He pulled her into his arms and they kissed hungrily. He then picked her up his arms and carried her to bed. They stayed there until morning.

All her fears temporarily gone, Claudia was happier. She and Attilio spent hours with their sons. The weather was cold, and snow sparkled in the winter sunshine.

One day they were out in the garden, all wrapped up warm, playing in the snow. The twins, now on their feet, were running about and squealing with excitement. Isabella was standing at a window watching. She felt a pang of guilt as she saw her sister-in-law's happy, radiant face as she played with her little sons, whom she obviously adored. Isabella had to admit then when Claudia was happy, she really was very beautiful. Isabella's sulky face grew more sullen. She would like to have been friends with her brother's pretty wife – but she was too afraid of her mother.

Christmas and New Year came and went. The Villa Carlotta, as usual, had been full of guests and life had been hectic.

By the time Attilio was due to leave for his tour of Australia, all Claudia's fears had returned. As he finished his packing she begged him, "Attiliio - can't we have a home of our own? Just a tiny place would do"

"No, Claudia. This is my home, and my family are here to look after you."

"But that's just it, they don't! I'm on my own all the time, and they hardly ever let me see Claudy and Tilly."

Attilio looked angry.

"Claudia - I hear enough - this is not true!"

She started to cry. She did not want to have a row with him just as he was leaving.

"I'm sorry," she wept.

"It is O.K. little one. Why you not go and visit your sister?"

"I'd like that," she sniffed, wiping her eyes.

"But you not take the twins." Claudia froze. Did he suspect she might take them and not bring them back?

"Of course not," she murmured. He smiled down at her.

"You not manage on your own - and they not have passports yet."

Of course - passports! She hadn't thought of that - what a fool she was!

Claudia and Attilio kissed good-bye, and hugged each other tightly.

As he made his way downstairs, she ran to the window overlooking the front of the house and waited for him to get to the car, which Bruno had ready waiting to take him to the airport.

Attilio reached the car, and as he opened the door he turned to wave at her. It had started to snow again. He smiled up at her through the falling flakes, and blew her a kiss.

He saw her lovely face looking down at him through the glass, not realising that he would never see her again . . .

FOUR

ESCAPE 1973

The Rossinis' hatred for Claudia grew more intense after Attilio had gone to Australia.

A week after his departure, Claudia bravely made her way to the nursery to try and see her sons. As she walked in, the old witch was standing by Claudio's cot. He was crying.

"Mama! Mama!" He put up his arms to Valeria, who picked him up.

Claudia's whole body was racked by a rage such as she had never known. She ran up to her mother-in-law and tried to take Claudy from her.

"He's my baby!" she screamed. "I am his Mama, not you!" Valeria glared at Claudia, her black eyes glittering. She tucked Claudy under her left arm, and with the back of her other hand she hit Claudia straight across her face, the large diamond ring on her finger catching Claudia's lip and making it bleed. Then opening the door, she pushed the shocked and trembling Claudia into the corridor and slammed the door behind her.

Claudia fell, gasping with shock, against the wall. She put a hand up to wipe the blood that was welling out of her lip. To make matters worse, she was suddenly confronted by Bruno.

She glared at him angrily.

"They are my babies!" she stormed. Bruno moved towards her and put his fat, sneering face close to hers, and a big, heavy leg between her trembling ones.

"No, not your babies - Rossini babies - family - Mafia... you understand?" She nodded wordlessly.

Frozen with shock, she just stared at him as he suddenly pulled out a knife with a wide blade out of his belt, moved it up to her face, then gently stroked her throat with it.

"Our babies... you understand?" he repeated threateningly.

Claudia was too frightened to move.

Bruno sneered at her, then gently removed the knife from her throat and put it back. Then, chuckling, he slowly walked away.

Claudia had never been so frightened in her whole life. When Bruno had gone, she made a dash for her rooms, sobbing. As she reached the small flight of steps, she tripped and fell, banging her shins. With tears streaming down her face, she limped into the living room, through into the bedroom, threw herself on to the bed and wept into the pillow.

"I want to go home," she cried to herself. "Mum, Dad, I need you so. Why did you have to die and leave me?" She cried herself to sleep.

The following morning produced another problem. As Claudia got out of bed, she felt sick and faint and a familiar cold sweat oozed out of her body. She staggered to the bathroom and vomited into the toilet. She knelt there, tears running down her ashen face.

"Oh, God," she whispered. "I'm pregnant again. I know I am, and I'm not going to let them get their hands on this baby!"

She eventually got herself back to bed and lay against the pillows, shivering, her eyes closed.

"I've got to get away from here as soon as I can, before anyone knows I'm pregnant," she thought fearfully. "What if I have another set of twins? I can't waste a moment.!"

She picked up the phone, and rang her sister.

"Colette?"

"No, she's not in," came the voice of another girl.

"When is she due back?"

"About lunchtime."

"Could you ask her to ring her sister as soon as she comes in? Please tell her it's urgent."

"Oh, it's you,Claudia. Of course I will."

Claudia thanked the girl and rang off.

She spent the morning lying in bed, waiting for the nausea to wear off. She felt so sick and afraid.

The phone suddenly rang. She snatched up the receiver to hear her sister's voice.

"Claudia, what's wrong? What's happened?"

"Oh, Colette, you've got to get me out of here as fast as you can. I've got to get away!" wept Claudia.

"Now calm down and tell me exactly what's happened."

Between sobs, Claudia told her sister everything.

"You're sure you're pregnant?"

"Yes, I'm certain."

"Look, Sis, are you prepared to walk out of that place with the clothes you stand up in and your passport?"

"Yes, I am."

"Good girl. Now I have a plan, but I have some phone calls and arrangements to make. I'll get back to you in a couple of days. I'll have to rescue you on my day off, as I never know where I'm flying to until I get to the airport, so I can't wait until I happen to fly to Italy, it will be too short notice."

"O.K. I'll wait."

"Good, now try to rest, and leave everything to me. I'll have you out of that place by the end of the week."

Claudia sighed with relief.

Later that day she got up and dressed and was pacing the floor nervously when she heard some banging and voices. She wondered what would be happening. When all went quiet she peeped out of the door, then cautiously walked down the corridor and turned the corner to the main landing. She caught her breath in shock, for on the door of the nursery was a brand new lock! She gently turned the handle, but the door would not open. She recoiled in shock and horror and ran back to her rooms.

"They've locked me out - I can't believe it! I may never see my babies again before I leave. What excuse will they give Attilio when he gets home? I expect they will have a good one," she thought to herself between sobs of misery.

The next couple of days dragged painfully by as Claudia waited for Colette to ring. What plan would she have? How was she going to get her away without the family knowing? She wondered when Attilio was going to ring. Being in Australia, their days and nights were opposite, and he certainly wasn't going to ring every day.

Colette's call finally came.

"Sis? You O.K.?"

"They've put a lock on the nursery door. I can't see Claudy and Tilly at all. I'll probably never see them again," Claudia wept.

"Do you still want out?"

"Yes. If I stay here much longer I'll have a nervous breakdown!"

"Right. Here's the plan."

"Go on."

"In two days time, that's Friday, I'll be arriving at Linati airport. You'll have to speak to Bruno and get him to drop you at the "Arrival" at 2 p.m. to meet me. Just walk in and I'll be there - leave the rest to me."

"But where will I go?"

"I'll tell you everything when I see you. Now you'll only be able to bring your handbag - make sure you've got your passport and all your English documents, your driving licence and so on."

"What about clothes and things?"

"I'll have a suitcase packed for you, don't worry."

"Colette, I'll have to leave Attilio a letter, I must explain."

"Of course you must, but bring it with you."

"But why?"

"So I can post it from somewhere, a long way from England. It will also stop anyone finding it and throwing it away."

"That's a great idea but where shall I address it? I can't send it here, Attilio won't be back until February."

"Do you have anyone who isn't family?"

Claudia thought for a moment. "Yes, his agent. I have his address!"

"Perfect. We'll send it to him and he can give it to Attilio."

"Yes, I'll do that."

"Now on Friday, what outdoor clothes will you be wearing?" Claudia frowned.

"Clothes....er...my brown leather coat with the hood, and my brown boots and bag."

"Right - now don't change your mind!"

"Colette, what's happening?"

"Claudia, my dear sister, I'm going to whisk you out of the country right under Bruno's big, fat nose, and how I would love to see him squirm when he has to tell Attilio that he lost you!"

"So would I," smiled Claudia weakly.

"I've got to go now, Sis. I'm truly sorry about that lock on the door. I've got to be honest, I am going to miss those boys, as much as you." Claudia's eyes filled with tears. "I'll ring you on Friday morning to check you're O.K. Bye, love, take care."

When Colette rang off, Claudia was shaking with fear and excitement. Two more days to go, and she would be out of here. Her heart ached at the thought of leaving her two little boys, but she couldn't take them with her - and she couldn't stay here any longer.

Her heart was pounding as she made her way downstairs to search for Bruno, passing the nursery on the way. She could hear Claudy and Tilly having tantrums, both crying lustily.

"That's it, boys," she thought grimly, "give them a hard time!"

When she found Bruno, "the Bulk" was in the kitchen, eating as usual.

"No wonder he's so fat," thought Claudia, looking at him nervously.

"Si?" he raised his eyebrows at her.

"My sister...mi sorella....come here (pointing to the floor) on Friday..venerdi...you understand?"

"Si."

"You take me to Linati airport... my sister arrive at 2 o'clock...due ora... you understand?"

"Si, we go l'una e un quarto... one and a quarter, OK?"

"Thank you... grazie."

He nodded.

Claudia turned and fled upstairs. She got to her room with a sigh of relief - the worst part was over, and if he wasn't there at 1.15, she would just have to get a taxi.

Feeling a little better after a sandwich, some wine and a couple of cigarettes, she started to sort out the things she would take with her. She still felt sick in the mornings, which only left her the rest of the day and the following afternoon and evening.

First of all she fetched her large, brown leather handbag, then she went through all the drawers and found her passport and driving licence, which were both still in her maiden name. She found her bank books and medical card - thank goodness her medical records were still in England!

When she had done this she looked round for photos to take with her. She selected a wedding photo - she and Attilio looking so radiant and happy – and a tear rolled down her cheek as she gazed at it solemnly. The rest of the photos would be of the twins. She took a lovely one of her and Attilio taken at Christmas with their sons. The boys were looking so grown-up with their big dark eyes shining under a fringe of black hair, and their wide smiles of tiny white teeth. She also chose a photo of Colette and herself taken at the christening. She hid the frames of the best photos in the drawer, to save room. Although she had collected quite a number of photos, she made sure she left some for Attilio.

She wrapped the photos carefully, and put them in the bag. She then went to another drawer to rescue some of the boys's baby clothes, selecting the first tiny outfits they had worn and their first little pairs of shoes. These were followed by the little arm bands they had worn in the hospital, with their names and birthweights on, and locks of their hair. Claudia wrapped these up carefully and added them to the bag.

"What about jewellery?" she thought to herself. She always wore the Gemini necklace and the gold bracelet Attilio had bought her for their first Chrstmas together. She rummaged through her jewellery box and picked up her mother's rings and gifts from her sister. She put a hand to her ears to feel the gold of her favourite earrings, another gift from her husband.

She looked round the room, and with a grim smile of satisfaction she threw into the bin, the Italian/English dictionary which "the Bulk" had given her for Christmas.

Claudia checked her bag. There was just enough room to add her make-up bag, brush, comb and cigarettes, which would go in at the last minute.

She then sat down and carefully wrote her farewell letter to her husband.

'Dear Attilio...'

By midday on Friday Claudia was a bag of nerves. Attilio had rung early the day before, sounding slightly drunk, and she guessed the cast were having a late night party. She had been so nervous she could hardly remember their conversation. All she could remember was bursting into tears after he had said 'goodbye'.

Claudia looked round their rooms - they were all clean and tidy for Attilio when he came home. She had even changed the bed and washing was hanging on a clothes-horse in the large bathroom. Her coat, shoes and bag were laid over an armchair. Colette had rung, and everything was going to plan.

Feeling too sick with worry to eat, Claudia made herself a mug of coffee and puffed her way through a couple of cigarettes. She then washed up the mug and ashtray, and started to get ready. She stood in front of the mirror to put on her coat over a brown cord skirt and warm, cream polo-neck sweater. Her hair looked pale and thin and her face was white, showing up the dark circles under her dull blue eyes.

Her coat done up, she put on her gloves and boots and

picked up her bag. With trembling legs she walked out of the room and down the stairs, passing the nursery with its new brass lock. She fought back the tears as she walked into the hall, and away from her two little children.

"I must be brave," she kept telling herself. "I musn't look back. I don't want Bruno to know what I'm doing."

Bruno was waiting for her, and without speaking they walked out to the car, leaving the Villa Carlotta behind. The day was extremely cold and she shivered as she got into the car. They drove in silence to the airport. Claudia staring straight ahead, her hands twisting in her lap. She was conscious of Bruno's big body next to hers. How she hated him! She felt quite sure that if she stayed here much longer he would probably have raped her.

When they drew up at the "Arrivals" door, Claudia got out hastily.

"I wait here," smirked Bruno, picking up a porno magazine. Claudia gave him a look of disgust, and hurried through the "Arrivals" door into the airport, which was humming with people.

She immediately spotted her sister, who was wearing a long cream coat and brown leather boots, and carrying a brown leather handbag, and a small blue suitcase. She ran up to her, and Colette grabbed her hand.

"Come on, through here." Colette dragged Claudia through a door marked "privato", and rushed her along some corridors.

"Where are we going?"

"Departures."

"What's happening?"

"We're going to change places - you're going to fly to England as me, and I'm going to fly to New York as you." Colette pushed open the door of a staff toilet, and dragged her sister in.

"We haven't much time. Your flight to Gatwick leaves in 40 minutes. Now give me your passport."

They exchanged passports.

"Now give me Attilio's letter, and I'll post it in New York. If he checks the airlines, he'll think you've gone to America, and when your letter arrives, it will hopefully convince him that you are there."

"But what about you?"

"I'll fly back tomorrow and join you."

"Where am I to go?"

Colette passed her an envelope. "In here is some English money. When you get to Gatwick, get a taxi to this hotel. It's a small place and I've booked you in under the name Veronica Smith, and you'll be a late departure on Saturday. You'll be paying cash so they won't want any identification or to see your credit card. You just wait there for me."

"But what if Attilio tries to contact you in London?" Claudia asked, alarm growing.

"He won't be able to contact me. It'll be some time before he knows what's happened, and I've swapped houses with another girl I know. If he phones up he'll be told I've moved and will not be given my address or phone number, and if he contacts the airport they won't give him the information either."

"Oh, Colette, you're so clever, you think of everything!"

"Now, Claudia, here are your flight tickets. I've booked you a smoking seat - and I've booked myself one on the flight to New York, just in case."

"Oh, Colette, thank you."

"Right," urged Colette, "now we change coats."

The two of them changed coats, and then Colette gently pushed her sister down on to a chair and, taking a brush out of her bag, brushed Claudia's hair up on to the top her head. Finally, taking the crocodile comb out of her own hair, she clasped Claudia's with it. Then she let down her own hair with a shake of her head, and brushed it quickly. She handed Claudia the small, blue suitcase.

"There's enough in here to be going on with until we can go shopping. Now, let's hurry."

They crept out of the ladies' toilet, and along more corridors, until they reached 'Departures'.

"Where will I go tomorrow, Colette? I can't stay in London."

"Don't worry, I've found you a perfect hideaway. I'll tell you about it tomorrow."

"O.K." Colette opened the door and showed her where to check in.

"Go straight through to the Departure Lounge when you've checked in," she urged."I'll see you tomorrow."

"Yes, and thanks for everything."

The two sisters hugged and kissed.

"Be careful," urged Claudia," in case Bruno comes looking for you."

"Don't worry, I have places to hide," smiled Colette, giving her sister a push.

With heart pounding and legs shaking, Claudia made her way to the check-in desk, where her case was weighed, labelled and whisked away. She then passed through the security check and into the 'duty-free' where she hastily bought cigarettes and a small bottle of brandy.

She soon found herself behind a group of people, all wandering along to the departure gate, chatting quietly.

Claudia felt uncomfortable with her hair piled up on top of her head. She felt so exposed that she pulled up the collar of her sister's coat to help hide her face.

She was relieved to get into the plane, and shrank into her window seat at the back. Fastening her seat belt, she looked anxiously out of the window, praying that Bruno wasn't hanging about, looking for her.

"Please hurry up," she silently begged the other passengers who were still milling about, shoving bags in the overhead lockers and settling themselves down.

Eventually everyone was settled. The 'seat belt' and 'no smoking' signs were lit up, and the stewardesses walked along the aisles checking bags were secure and everyone was strapped in.

The plane, at last, began to move. "Hurry, please hurry," Claudia though to herself.

As the aircraft slowly taxied towards the runway, the stewardesses went through the emergency procedures, and then took their seats. The voice of the captain greeted them all, and wished everyone a comfortable journey.

The plane stopped. Claudia began to panic.

"Oh, God, no!" she thought frantically, "what if Bruno has discovered where I am, and they ask me to get off? Or, even worse, he might be getting on!"

Her fears were unfounded, for the plane began to move slowly along the runway. Claudia clutched her bag with its precious contents, and her other hand went up to her Gemini necklace. Then, with a roar, the plane sped along the runway at terrific speed - the nose went up, and they rose gently into the air.

Claudia sighed with relief. The plane rose and eventually levelled off. She looked out of the window and gazed at the sea of white clouds which stretched into eternity. As soon as the 'no smoking' signs went out, she gratefully lit a cigarette. The drinks trolley arrived and she bought a small bottle of white wine.

She sat quietly thinking.

"I've got away, I'm free." She tried not to think about her husband and children, and blinked away the tears that were filling her eyes.

After picking at her meal, she drank her coffee and smoked another cigarette. When the trays had been taken away, she lay back her head and closed her eyes, trying to shut away the world. She was going home.

By the time Bruno had realised that his sister-in-law had completely disappeared, Claudia was halfway across the English Channel.

FIVE

HIDEAWAY 1973

By the time Claudia arrived at her hotel, it was dark and cold. She checked in under her false name and went up to her room, which was a twin. It was warm and comfortable with a T.V. in a corner near the window and a tea-tray on the dressing table. The bathroom was small but clean with white, fluffy towels laid neatly over the rail.

With a sigh she laid the small suitcase on one of the beds and opened it up. Inside were two pairs of jeans, two sweaters, a nightdress, some underwear, a pair of shoes and a bag of toiletries. Tucked away underneath were two packets of dry biscuits to ease her morning sickness and a packet of 200 cigarettes. Dear Colette - she thought of everything.

Claudia switched on the kettle and the T.V. and while the kettle was boiling she took off her coat and boots. A few minutes later she was sitting on the bed with a couple of biscuits, a hot cup of tea, her cigarettes and an ashtray on the bedside table.She sat there wondering what was happening at the Villa Carlotta. Bruno must have returned there by now. Had Attilio phoned? What had they told him? How worried would he be? What would he do? Her stomach churned with anxiety as she thought about Claudy and Tilly. They would never remember her. Tears welled up in her eyes.

She eventually got herself undressed and put on the pretty nightdress her sister had bought her. She took out of her bag a photo of her two little boys. She looked at it sadly. "Goodnight, my little ones," she whispered as she kissed the photo and then placed it on the bedside table. She turned out the light, lay down and cried herself to sleep.

The following day Claudia waited anxiously for her sister. Her little case was packed, and she sat drinking tea, then coffee and smoking, listening intently for the knock on the door.

It was 5 p.m. before Colette arrived with her good friend, Rachel Harris. Colette looked tired after her long journey to New York and back within 24 hours.

The two sisters hugged each other and Colette introduced Claudia to her friend.

"Claudia, this is Rachel, and it's through her that we've found somewhere for you to live."

"Oh, thank you," smiled Claudia shyly.

"We'll set off now and we'll tell you everything on the way," added Colette.

"Don't you both want something to eat and drink?" asked Claudia.

"We'll get out of London and stop on the way for a break."

"O.K."

The three of them left the hotel and got into Rachel's car. Colette turned to Claudia.

"Rachel is driving, as she knows the way and hasn't lost a night's sleep, like me," she grinned.

They set off, Rachel driving confidently through the busy London streets, which were brightly lit against a dark cloudy sky.

"I'm still worried in case Attilio sends someone after you, Colette."

"Don't worry, Sis, it's all fixed. I told you I'd swapped houses and the girls I've been sharing with promised me that if he keeps bothering them they'll say we've both gone to America. That should stop him."

"But he might see you at one of the airports in London or Italy one day!"

"No he won't," grinned Colette. "I'm transferring to the Midlands, to Birmingham airport, and doing long-haul flights."

"Birmingham? But why?"

"Because the place I've found for you is in the Midlands, and I can be nearer to you."

"But where am I going?"

"To a tiny village called Bishops Fell."

"Where's that?"

"It's near a town called Cropwell, which is on the borders of Warwickshire and Leicestershire."

"How did you find it?"

"Well, Rachel comes from Cropwell, and she has an older brother called Bill, who has a building business. Now Bill knows the area very well and he's found a tiny cottage tucked away out of sight from the road. The lady who owns it has recently got married and moved into her husband's house, and instead of selling her cottage, she;s decided to rent it out."

"It sounds just right," sighed Claudia.

"There's more good news," interrupted Rachel. "The cottage next door is lived in by a very nice lady, who's a retired nurse. She's a widow and spends a lot of time looking after her grandchildren, so although she's usually out during the day, she's in during the evenings and weekends. Her name is Maureen James, and she is really nice. She's not a nosey-parker, but if you need any help or want someone to talk to, she'll come round."

"That sounds perfect."

"I'm sure you'll like it, Sis."

"I don't care if it's a tumbledown shack, so long as it hides me away."

"Tonight, Claudia, you and I are going to stay at the Kings Head pub in Bishops Fell, and Rachel and Bill will join us for a meal. Bill has the keys to the cottage, which is called May Cottage, and he'll take us round tomorrow morning to see it. If you want the cottage, he'll take you to the estate agents on Monday morning to make the arrangements."

"That sounds wonderful, I'm so grateful."

"It's no trouble, Sis, you know that."

"How long can you and Rachel stay?"

"We both have to be back by Monday evening, as we both have flights at the crack of dawn on Tuesday. So after you've been to the estate agents we'll take you round Cropwell so that you can get some shopping and new clothes."

"Honestly, Colette, you think of everything. What would I do without you?"

Once they were out of London, the three of them stopped for a break and a coffee, then set off for Bishops Fell.

They arrived at 8.30. All Claudia could see through the car windows was tall swaying trees, thick hedgerows and stone cottages, with the warm glow of lights shining through curtains.

They pulled up in the car park of the Kings Head and eased themselves out of the car. It was now very windy and Claudia shivered as she and her sister collected their cases from the boot of the car. They made their way to the large oak door, Claudia pushing her wind-blown hair out of her eyes. They entered the pub and were greeted by the landlady, who knew Rachel.

Colette and Claudia were sharing a twin room, and after introductions were made, the three of them climbed the old, highly polished wooded staircase to the twins' room, so they could freshen up.

"Where will you be staying, Rachel?" asked Claudia.

"With my brother. He's living in the family home. Our parents are dead now. Bill has actually bought a deserted, old pub on Cropwell Hill, and he's renovating it and turning it into a house. When he finally finishes it, which will be some time, he'll move in and we'll sell the family house and share the money."

"Will you live with your brother?"

"Not really. I live in London anyway, but the house Bill is doing up will have at least four bedrooms, so I can always stay with him when I visit."

"That'll be nice."

The girls reached their room. Colette unlocked the door and switched on the light. The room was large with a low ceiling and dark red velvet curtains were drawn across the window.

Each side of the window were two single beds, which were covered with red patterned bedspreads, and a set of folded white towels were set at the bottom of each one. There was a large,oak wardrobe and dressing-table, two armchairs and a coffee table with a tea-tray. On the right was a large old-fashioned fireplace with an electric fire, and on the left was a small handbasin attached to the wall. The bathroom and toilet were in the corridor opposite.

"This looks cosy!" exclaimed Colette, as she and her twin laid their cases on the beds. The three of them freshened up and made their way downstairs.

The Kings Head was a very old pub. In the centre was an enormous fireplace with a roaring log fire. The dining room was on one side and the bar on the other. The girls made their way into the bar, which was busy, to await the arrival of Rachel's brother. They found a table and while Rachel went to the bar to get drinks, Claudia and Colette looked round.

The walls and floor were of old grey stone. The ceiling was low with heavy oak beams. The curtains were drawn across mullioned windows, and horse brasses and pictures of horses and huntsmen decorated the walls. An old copper tub filled with logs stood in the fireplace, where flames crackled and spat out a glowing warmth. The large tables and chairs were also made of dark oak.

Rachel brought over three glasses of wine and Claudia, who was beginning to feel nervous again, lit a cigarette with shaking fingers. She looked across at Rachel, a very tall girl with short beautifully cut brown hair, large grey eyes and a wide smiling mouth.

"W-what time will your brother be here?" stammered Claudia, praying that he would not look like Attilio.

"About nine. I've booked a table, and we'll eat as soon as he gets here. I wish he'd hurry up, I'm famished!"

Rachel's brother arrived a few minutes later, and he was nothing like Attilio. Bill Harris was a gentle giant, standing at 6' 4" with big shoulders, and arms and legs like tree trunks. His hair, the same colour as Rachel's, was cut short with a side parting, a few strands falling over thick eyebrows, which were raised over serious grey eyes. His nose was slightly crooked over a mouth like his sister's, wide, warm and smiling.

Bill walked up to the table with long strides, and was introduced to the twins. When Bill was introduced to Claudia, his eyes took in the sight of this beautiful, sad girl, with her golden hair framing a white face, and dark rings circling her frightened blue eyes. His whole body was swept with a great feeling of sympathy, and he wanted to take her in his arms and hold her tight. Instead, he merely shook her hand, his grey eyes almost devouring her.

"Come on, let's eat!" said Rachel, grabbing her brother's arm. The four of them made their way into the dining area, and sat at a table near the roaring fire.

Claudia found herself sitting with Bill on her right, Colette on her left and Rachel opposite. She was very conscious of the huge man sitting next to her, and she was overcome with an urge to tuck her small hand into his large, weatherbeaten one. He looked so strong and capable, and handsome in a rugged sort of way, in his dark trousers and thick cream sweater. A blush crept into her cheeks.

The waitress brought over the menus and they poured over them while she fetched them drinks - a beer for Bill and wine for the girls. Everyone ordered steak - Bill and Colette chose chips and peas with theirs and Claudia and Rachel chose a jacket potato and salad.

Colette patted Claudia's arm.

"Now make sure you eat it up - you're much too thin, and you must think of the baby."

"O.K. Sis."

They all chatted while they waited for their meals, though Claudia sat silently some of the time, smoking and gazing into the fire.

Eventually their meals arrived, which they all enjoyed, followed by coffee. When they had finished, Colette yawned.

"Well, I'm off to bed. I'm bushed!"

They all got up and said their goodbyes.

"We'll meet you here at eleven in the morning," said Rachel.

"O.K. Rachel. Thanks and goodnight."

Bill and Rachel left and the two sisters made their way upstairs. By the time Claudia had got herself ready for bed, Colette was fast asleep.

So as not to wake her sister, Claudia turned out the light, and slipped silently into her bed. She snuggled down, listening to the wind howling outside, and thinking about her life. Would she ever be able to forgive herself for the terrible thing she had done? Leaving the husband and children she loved because she had been frightened and unhappy? Tears rolled silently down her face, and her body shook with muffled sobs.

When Claudia woke the next morning she found her sister standing by her bed with a cup of tea and a couple of dry biscuits.

"Here you are, love. Have these to help that morning sickness. I'm going downstairs for a cooked breakfast."

"Ugh!"

"See you later," grinned Colette as she left the room.

At 11 O'clock. the two girls went downstairs to find Bill and Rachel waiting.

"It's not far to May Cottage, " said Rachel, "and it's quite a nice morning, Shall we walk?" Everyone agreed.

They left the pub and made their way down the Cropwell Road. Claudia looked round at the pretty village bathed in wintry sunshine. A village of pretty stone cottages, a very old church and a small school. Horse-riders clip-clopped past them and smiled. Claudia felt her spirits begin to lift.

After a few minutes' walk they crossed the road and went down a little lane.

"This is Fox Cub Lane," said Bill. "Down here is a small pub called the Fox Cub. If you ever get a car yourself, you'll be allowed to park it in the car park. It's a friendly little place and does nice meals at lunchtime and in the evening, if you don't want to cook."

"That's handy," replied Claudia.

When they passed the Fox Cub, they came to a row of small cottages.

"We go down here," said Bill, suddenly turning down a small alleyway between two of the cottages. They followed Bill down the alley with its uneven floor of old grey bricks. The alley veered to the left, then to the right. There were high fences on either side, with dark green conifers peeping over the top. Ahead of them was Cropwell Wood.

At the end of the alley they turned right to find a pathway with two attached cottages on the right-hand side, with grey stone walls, a small window facing the woods and a wooden door with tubs of brightly coloured pansies either side. On the left was a border of shrubs, a wooden fence and beyond that a grassy path winding its way alongside the wood, which, in the spring, would be filled with bluebells.

"Goodness!" exclaimed Colette. "This place would take some finding!"

Claudia's heart was pounding. It was a perfect hideaway!

Bill fished the keys out of his pocket, opened the door and they all filed in. The door opened straight into the living room, which was small, plain and comfortable with a stone fireplace on the right and a window at the other end looking out over a small back garden.

The walls and carpet were in cream with narrow beams across the ceiling. There was a cream-coloured, flowered three-piece suite, a TV, a coffee table and a small wooden sideboard.

At the bottom of the room were two doors. The one on the left led into a small but well-fitted kitchen with a door leading to the back garden. The door on the right led to a winding staircase which led up to two bedrooms, one of them very small, and a small bathroom. Bill spoke to Claudia.

"The lady who owns the cottage has left almost everything, so you won't have to worry about getting crockery, towels or bed linen."

Claudia stood and looked down onto the back garden, which had a small lawn, a few bedraggled plants, conifers on the right peeping over the alley, a small shed in one corner and a drooping washing line. She looked across at the the back of the cottage facing her on the other side of the fence.

"You won't be overlooked," said Bill at her shoulder. "An old lady lives there and she doesn't use the back bedroom. Will it be alright for you?" he added hopefully.

"It's perfect. Thank you very much."

The following morning Bill took Claudia and Colette to the estate agents in Cropwell, where she signed an agreement, gave a cheque for a month's rent in advance, and was given the keys. Bill then took them to May Cottage and showed Claudia how to set the central heating, use the washing machine and light the gas fire. He also gave her his phone number.

"If you need anything at all, just ring me."

"You're very kind, thank you."

Bill, Claudia and Colette then met Rachel for lunch and the three girls went shopping to get Claudia some more clothes and buy food for her new home.

"There's a small shop in Bishops Fell if you need anything, but things will be dearer there than in the supermarkets. If you ring Bill, he'll take you shopping," smiled Rachel.

"You've all been so kind," said Claudia, her eyes filling with tears.

Colette and Rachel stayed at the cottage until it was time to go back to London.

"I'll visit you whenever I can," said Colette, hugging her sister, "and when I move to Birmingham I'll stay with you on my days off."

"Oh, Colette, what would I do without you!" cried Claudia.

May Cottage was like a rabbit hutch compared with the Villa Carlotta, but Claudia loved it. She cleaned and polished and bought plants and silk flowers, and some pictures to put on the wall. Her little home became warm and cosy and safe. She met her neighbour. Maureen James, a small, plump grey-haired lady with a ready smile, and the two of them would often chat together over a coffee.

Colette paid regular visits, and they would go out together for meals and shopping, buying things for the baby and the cottage, and more clothes for Claudia.

Bill was very good to Claudia and they became good friends. He would take her shopping and do odd jobs for her, and they would sit and chat to each other. She told him all about her life with Attilio and about her fears, and he told her about his young wife who had died only 18 months after their marriage, He had sold their home with everything in it, and moved back with his parents, who a short while later had also died. He now only had his sister and a cousin, Simon.

By March, Claudia was happily settled. Bill would now come round on a Sunday morning if Colette wasn't there, and mow her lawn and tidy the small garden, which was now bursting with colourful tulips and daffodils. Claudia would then cook him a delicious Sunday lunch. After lunch he would help her wash up, and then go home so that she could rest, as she was always falling asleep in the afternoons.

Bill had also helped Claudia to get a car, and she was now the proud owner of a second-hand silver Mini.

She was now three months pregnant.

"I must see a doctor," she said to Colette on one of her visits.

"Yes, you must."

"I don't want anyone else to know about Claudy and Tilly. I've only told Bill. Do you think the doctor will be able to tell that I've had a baby before?"

"I doubt it. You had a normal birth, so you won't have a scar or anything."

"I hate telling lies. but if I tell the doctor, he'll want to know everything - I couldn't face it."

"I don't blame you - your past is best kept a secret. Just the thought of the Mafia is enough to give anyone a nightmare!"

"I know. Every time I see someone who looks like an Italian I shake with fear and scuttle back here. If his family find me, Colette, they won't need to cut my throat – I'd die of fright anyway."

"Don't worry, Sis, they won't find you here."

"I know, but I'm still scared. Even when I see the postman come by with the mail, I'm scared he'll drop a letter through my door, but all I'm getting at the moment is leaflets and bills, thank God!"

Claudia registered with a local doctor, and he confirmed her pregnancy, giving her a due date in the middle of September. Her medical records were sent for from her previous doctor in Boreham Wood. She was greatly relieved to know that she was not having another set of twins!

The weeks and months flew by. Colette had now bought herself a charming flat in Solihull in Birmingham and visited her sister on her days off. She was now doing long-haul flights, so that she would never be in Italy. This also gave her three days off at a time.

Claudia was looking forward to having her baby, and being able to look after it herself. She had no wicked in-laws now to take her child from her. She found, also, that she was not as big and so was able to get about much better than she did before. On summer days she would sit in her pretty little garden, and in the evenings she would sit in her lounge knitting baby clothes.

Some summer evenings she would go to bed early. She liked to sit up in bed and watch the sun set through the leafy trees facing her window. Every night she would kiss a photo of her two little boys, and then put it back into the drawer of the bedside cabinet, in case anyone saw it. She had shown the photo to Bill, but not to Maureen, and was worried that her neighbour might come up here for some reason and see it. Maureen had still not been told about Claudy and Tilly.

When Claudia's baby was nearly due, Bill phoned every day and came to sit with her every evening in case her labour started and she was alone. Unknown to Claudia, Bill had taken on a manager, so that he could have more time to spend with her.

Bill was, by now, deeply in love with Claudia, and would have done anything to protect her.

Claudia's baby was born on 15th September. She gave birth to a beautiful, dark-haired little daughter.

She named her little girl, Lucy, after her mother.

SIX

ANOTHER LIFE FOR CLAUDIA 1973-1977

Bill had stayed with Claudia through her confinement, and wearing a mask and gown, he had sat beside her and held her hand while she gave birth to Lucy.

Bill's grey eyes had filled with tears as he saw the look on Claudia's face at the sight of her little daughter.

"Isn't she beautiful, Bill?"

"As beautiful as her mother," he replied, huskily.

"She looks like Attilio with all this black hair," whispered Claudia. "Please, God, don't ever let him find her and take her away from me."

After Lucy's birth, Bill rang Colette with the news, and the next day she was down to visit, her eyes sparkling and her arms full of pretty dresses for her niece.

"Oh, Claudia, she's absolutely gorgeous!"

"She looks like Attilio."

"She's only got his black hair, now don't worry."

Colette stayed with Claudia for two weeks, and the two of them drooled over Lucy. Maureen popped round to see the baby and brought gifts, then went away with Claudia's washing.

"Maureen's such a good neighbour."

"Yes, she is. You've been very lucky to find this placc. I'm so pleased for you."

Knowing what a dreadful time Claudia had had trying to look after her little boys, Colette made sure that her sister spent all her time with Lucy, while she looked after them, cooking and cleaning. When Lucy cried the two sisters did take it turns to nurse her to sleep. One day, as Colette was gazing adoringly at Lucy, Claudia smiled at her.

"Colette, don't you ever want to marry and have children?"

"Of course I do, but I'm not ready yet. Anyway I'm too busy looking after you!" she laughed.

Although the small bedroom had been turned into a nursery, Lucy slept in a cradle next to Claudia and a camp bed had been put in the nursery for Colette to sleep on, instead of her sleeping on the settee.

One afternoon, while Lucy was sleeping, the sisters were chatting.

"When are you going to register her birth, Sis?"

"I don't know. I don't know what to put on the birth certificate."

"You could register her as Lucy Morris."

"Yes, I know, but I don't want to have to put 'father unknown' on it. I don't want Lucy to think she's illegitimate, and start asking me who her father is when she gets older."

"Mmmm... I tell you what you could do."

"What's that?"

"Well, you could register her as Lucy Morris and give Attilio's name as the father, and then you could buy a short birth certificate, which you could give her when she gets older. If she grows up like other children she'll not even bother to ask."

"What's the difference?"

"The difference? A lot. A short birth certificate just gives the name of the child plus date and place of birth. There are no parents' names on it at all."

"Of course, but when she gets older she might ask about her father. What shall I say?"

"You'll have to tell her he's dead."

"Yes, I will. It's the only way. I can't have her searching for him."

"No, she must never do that!"

Claudia looked down at her tiny daughter with her smooth olive skin and mop of soft, dark hair. "I just hope and pray she never wants to sing."

"You must stop her if she does, Claudia. We can't have her becoming a singer and meeting Attilio. She could lead him to you."

"I know. It's a terrifying thought."

"Will you ever tell her the truth?"

"I don't want to, but I'll have to see what kind of person she turns out to be, and whether I can trust her to keep such a secret."

Colette smiled. "Of course, you might marry again. If you do, Lucy would have a father - and she'll probably never know he's not her real father."

"What are you trying to say?"

"Oh, come off it, Claudia - you must know that Bill is madly in love with you, and he already adores Lucy."

"I know, but it's too soon for me to think of anyone else yet, and I still love Attilio," Claudia replied sadly.

Before Colette left, Claudia drove into Cropwell to register Lucy's birth. She came away with a short birth certificate. It was a great relief to have a short one without the parents' names on it. Deep in her heart, she was glad she had given Attilio's name as the father. She felt it was only fair to him. He would have loved Lucy so. Tears of sadness ran down her face when she thought of the lovely daughter she had denied him. She imagined his face lighting up at the sight of her, and his rich sexy voice saying, "My little Claudia, what a clever girl you are to give me this beautiful daughter!"

By the time she got back to May Cottage, she was breaking her heart.

"Claudia, what's wrong?" asked Colette, her blue eyes anxious.

"It's nothing," sobbed Claudia. "It's just baby blues."

Colette put an arm round her sister. "Come and sit down, love, and I'll get you a brandy and a fag."

"Thanks, Colette." Claudia grabbed some tissues and began wiping her eyes and nose. She then lit a cigarette and sipped the brandy. Lucy started to cry.

"Would you feed her please, Colette?" Claudia was feeling so racked with guilt, she could hardly look at Lucy.

Colette warmed Lucy's bottle, then picked up the crying baby. She sat well away from Claudia's smoke, put Lucy's bib on her, nestled her in her arm, and gave her the bottle. Lucy settled happily.

Colette left the following morning, glad that her sister had got over her fit of the 'blues'.

Claudia settled down to a new life with Lucy. Bill was a constant visitor and he adored Lucy. He would play with her and nurse her when she was poorly, and buy her everything she needed.

Lucy grew up a happy, loving child, and was calling Bill 'dada' before she was a year old. She grew up contented and loved animals and babies, and would spend most of her time pushing her favourite doll round the tiny cottage and garden in its little pram. She also grew up very beautiful, with her large brown eyes, long, black swinging hair and a pretty mouth.

By the time she was two, Lucy was asking, "Where Daddy?" and would throw herself at Bill whenever he walked in the door.

"Do you mind her calling me Daddy?" he asked Claudia one day.

"Of course not, she loves you."

"I love her, too, as if she were my own."

"I know."

Bill swallowed. He loved Claudia and wanted to ask her to live with him, but he was always afraid she would refuse, and their friendship would be spoiled.

By the time Lucy was almost three Claudia was feeling more content than she had ever done. She was kept busy with her lively, energetic daughter. She had more of a social life and Maureen would often baby-sit so that she could go out with Bill or Colette when she came to visit. Lucy would be starting play-school in September, and Bill had offered Claudia a part-time job in his offices if she wanted it, so that she could earn some money. Claudia was looking forward to it, and her confidence was growing.

But one night something happened to shatter her life once again.

It was a summer's evening. Colette had gone home earlier as she was flying the next morning. Lucy was asleep upstairs. The summer sun had sneaked behind dark clouds and rain was in the air.

Instead of sitting in the garden, Claudia settled herself, comfortably on the settee, a glass of wine on the coffee table, a cigarette in her hand. She tried not to smoke in front of Lucy, but would light up as soon as her daughter had gone to bed.

With the remote control in her hand, she flicked over the T.V.channels and found that a chat programme was just starting. The guests were a famous footballer, a comedienne and the new singing sensation from America called Tony Ross. She settled down to watch it.

Although Claudia rarely watched the news or read a paper, she had heard of Tony Ross, but had not seen his picture.

When the comedienne had finished her chat with the presenter, he introduced Tony Ross. A great cheer went up from the audience as he walked on, dark and handsome. The camera zoomed in on his smiling face. Claudia nearly fainted with shock.

"Oh, no!" she gasped. "Attilio! Oh my God!"

Claudia felt weak with shock and her legs began to shake. She sat mesmerised like a frightened rabbit, watching him talking and laughing. It was just like he was sitting there in her living room. He eventually got up to sing. The music began to play and he started to sing one of his favourite Mario Lanza songs. Her heart began to pound, and the blood in her veins ran cold. When he had finished, the audience cheered and he sang another song - one of her favourites. Was he singing it for her? The tears ran unheeded down her pale face.

Suddenly the telephone rang. Claudia nearly leapt out of her skin. She stared at it in horror - could it be one of the Rossinis? Had they found her? With a shaking hand she eventually picked up the receiver.

"Claudia!" It was Colette. "Are you alright?"

Claudia was crying.

"Have you seen him?"

"Yes."

"Claudia, don't cry. It's O.K."

"It's such a shock, seeing him there."

"I know, I switched on a few minutes ago. I didn't know he'd gone to America."

"Nor me. It... it... didn't occur to me. Do you think he went there looking for me?"

"I don't know, Sis. He could have done, but America's a big place."

"Is this programme live?"

"Yes."

"That means he's in London. Oh, Colette, I'm so scared!"

"He doesn't know where you are, Sis."

"I know, but he's so near."

"I wish I could be with you."

"So do I, but you have to fly tomorrow, and you mustn't get into trouble by coming back here."

"Why don't you ask Bill to come round."

"No. no....I don't want him to know. It wouldn't be fair on him to see Attilio's face on T.V. and in the newspapers and know he's my husband."

"What are you going to do?"

"Get drunk and go to bed!"

"Don't be silly. What if Lucy wakes up?"

"I won't get that drunk!"

The two girls chatted for some time, and when Claudia returned to the settee, the programme had finished.

Claudia downed a couple of brandies, then made her way up to her bedroom. She lay listening to the heavy summer rain pounding the window. The weather had turned as miserable as she felt. She was so frightened she could not sleep, but lay tossing and turning until morning.

During the next few days Claudia was so nervous and frightened after seeing Attilio on the T.V. that she refused to leave the house. She told Maureen she felt unwell, and her neighbour went out and fetched her some shopping.

Claudia's greatest fear was of Attilio finding Lucy and taking her away.

"He must never find her - never!" she told herself firmly. She was also paranoid about Lucy ever wanting to sing, so she never played any music in the house or let Lucy watch programmes on the T.V. which contained music and singing.

She knew this fear would never go away.

Colette returned a few days later to find her sister looking pale and tired.

"Now, Claudia, don't worry, he's gone back to America."

"Are you sure?"

"Yes. I was chatting to someone on the plane who's a great fan of his. Apparantly Attilio does live permanently in America - he went there when he was offered a contract about three years ago, and decided to stay. He's very discreet about his personal life, and rarely does interviews - when he does he'll only talk about his career."

"Oh, so no-one knows about me?"

"It looks that way."

"I still don't trust his family. The Mafia - they always want revenge," Colette continued. "According to this 'fan' Tony Ross is adored by everyone, and has hordes of women after him wherever he performs. I'm sorry, Sis."

"I knew this would happen," said Claudia softly. "If I'd stayed in Milan, I would have been stuck with his family, and he would be travelling about enjoying himself - I would have hated it." She looked down at Lucy. "I know I did the right thing to leave him. I could never have accepted him being unfaithful to me all the time. I should never have married him."

"But you did love him, Claudia, and I know he loved you."

"I know, but I followed my heart instead of my head."

"Never mind, Sis, it's all over now, and you have a new life."

"Yes, I have. I must be sensible and try to forget the past." She started to cheer up. "Colette, I'm going to change my image."

"What are you going to do?"

"Have my hair cut - it will make me look different."

So Colette drove them into Cropwell and looked after Lucy while Claudia went to the hairdressers. She came out an hour and a half later, looking a new woman. Her shoulder-length hair had been cut into a bob which fell just below her ears, and she now had a fringe which enhanced her big blue eyes.

"You look lovely!" exclaimed Colette, "and it really suits you."

Claudia smiled happily. Her pale, thin face now looked rounder and prettier with her new hairstyle.

"If Attilio saw you now, he wouldn't recognise you."

"Good," replied Claudia.

As the months rolled by, Claudia tried hard to forget the past and make her daughter's life as happy as she could. She turned down Bill's offer of a job, as she still felt safer being at home.

One warm, sunny day in August, just before Lucy's fourth birthday, Bill and Claudia took Lucy to the nearby park. Lucy loved the park and being with other children. They watched her playing with another little girl, a bit smaller than herself.

"She loves other children," smiled Claudia.

"It's a shame she hasn't got a brother or sister," replied Bill tentatively.

"Yes, it is."

"You could remedy that, Claudia." He looked down at her and she blushed, a nervous hand going up to touch her Gemini necklace which she still wore.

She then looked up at him and smiled. "What are you suggesting, Bill?"

"I'm suggesting," he said slowly," that you come and live with me as my wife. I know you can't marry me, but we could live together. Lucy already thinks I'm her father - and we could give her a brother or sister." Claudia suddenly laughed.

"Oh, Bill, I thought you'd never ask!"

"Really? Oh, Claudia!" His face lit up with joy, and he put an arm round her shoulders.

"Look," he said eagerly, "the house I've been renovating on Cropwell Hill is finished - it just needs to be decorated and furnished. Let's go up there now and show Lucy her new home, and then, tomorrow we can start looking round for furniture and things, and you can choose whatever you want."

"Oh, Bill, you're so good to me. Yes, let's go!"

"Lucy!" called Bill. She looked over, ran up to him and threw herself into his arms.

"Come on, sweetheart, we're going to look at our new house." The three of them set off to Cropwell Hill, a beautiful place of farms and houses, green fields and trees overlooking a winding river, of sheep and cows grazing in peace and tranquillity. The old inn that was now Bill's home had been called the The Chimney Pots and Bill had changed it to Chimneys.

Chimneys was situated on the lower slopes of Cropwell Hill. They drove up a winding lane of trees and blackberry bushes, past Gage's Farm and came to a stop on the top of a rise, which consisted of Chimneys, some stone cottages, a small, very old church, a general store and a large pub called The White Horse. The original inn had been used as a bar and small lounge, with a new extension at the back, which was a restaurant looking out onto a landscape of greenery and where, on dark nights, the lights of the distant towns twinkled on the horizon.

Bill, Claudia and Lucy got out of the car and looked at Bill's large house, Lucy jumping up and down in excitement. Chimneys was shaped like a large letter E with the middle bar missing. The main part of the building, facing the road, was the living room, with the kitchen going down on the right and the dining room on the left, facing the back garden. There was a double garage at the side.

Upstairs were five bedrooms and two bathrooms, and on top of the thatched roof were two tall chimneys. The windows were all diamond-paned and sparkled in the sunshine.

"It looks lovely," smiled Claudia. Lucy grabbed Bill's hand.

"Come on, Daddy, come on!"

Laughing, Bill opened the large wooden front door, and they all filed in, their footsteps echoing on the bare floorboards. They were standing in the living room, which had a door on the right leading to the kitchen and a window with a window seat, opposite looking on to the back garden. On the left was a door leading to the dining room and,like the Kings Head in Bishops Fell, there was a huge fireplace also leading into the dining room. Lucy immediately ran through it and back again, and with her eyes wide with surprise, she looked up into the huge chimney.

"That's where Father Christmas will be coming down," grinned Bill. He turned to Claudia. "I'll put a gas fire in here, one of those that look real, and I'll put a fire-guard on either side."

"That's a relief," she replied.

The dining room was long with a window at each end, and in the far corner was a flight of winding stairs leading up to a landing which ran alongside the house, with another set of stairs leading down to a corner of the kitchen. The bedrooms all led off the landing. Bill showed Claudia all the rooms and then they made their way down to a fully-fitted kitchen, with a window also at each end - a door leading into the garage and a door leading into the garden. He took Claudia's hand.

"Come and see this," He led her over to the staircase in the corner of the kitchen, and pressed a wooden panel. A door under the stairs slid open to reveal a staircase winding down below the house.

"I've converted the old cellars - come and see." Bill led Claudia and Lucy down until they came face to face with an underground set of rooms, all clean and freshly painted. Bill looked down at Claudia.

"Down here is a bathroom, bedroom, lounge and tiny kitchen. It can be used for Lucy to play in, or for visitors or for your sister to stay in. It can also be used as a hideaway, if any sinister-looking Italians are prowling about - you can stay down here and hide."

Claudia looked up at him in amazement.

"Bill, this is wonderful, but I don't want to get you in any danger because of me!"

"Don't worry, I'm not afraid. Anyway, Italian men are only half the size of me," he grinned.

"Bill, you're so good to me, I don't know what to say."

Bill put an arm round her shoulders and whispered in her ear. "I love you, Claudia. I know you don't love me, but I have enough love for both of us."

She buried her head in his shoulder.

"Mummy, Daddy. come on!" cried Lucy.

Bill smiled. "Let's go and see the garden, shall we?"

"Yes, yes!" shouted Lucy, and raced up the stairs to the kitchen, and out into the garden.

When they got outside, Bill showed them round the large garden. Immediately outside was a large patio, where Bill was going to put a garden table and chairs, and tubs of flowers. Beyond this was a garden of mixed shrubs and flowers, with winding paths of crazy paving weaving in and out. Lucy was soon running in and out of the shrubbery and squealing with delight. The rest of the garden, which was lawned, sloped down to the river. The banks of the river were steep and lined with trees, fenced off with large, black wrought iron fencing, to stop anyone falling into the river, and to stop anyone from outside getting in. Soon all three of them were standing peering through the metal bars at the water far below, rushing over stones. The water was clear and sparkling as is was caught by the rays of sun that fought their way through the leafy branches.

"What a lovely view," murmured Claudia.

The rest of the garden was surrounded by a high stone wall, beyond shrubs and trees.

"Well, what do you think?" asked Bill.

"I think it's wonderful, Bill, and I shall feel so safe here."

During the next few weeks, Bill and Claudia went out shopping for furniture, carpets and curtains. Out of the money left to her by her parents, she bought the bed linen and crockery and all the trimmings, such as pictures, ornaments and plants. Bill also bought Lucy a swing and slide for the garden.

By the October Chimneys was ready for them all to move in. Lucy loved her new home and spent hours pushing her doll's pram in and out or all the rooms and running up and down the two flights of stairs.

Once they had settled in, Bill and Claudia decided to have a house-warming party. On the Saturday morning, Maureen, who was now called Nanny by Lucy, came round to help and was going to stay the night. Colette and Rachel arrived later and would stay the weekend. Colette had had her hair cut like her sister's, and they were once again identical! Also invited was Bill's cousin, Simon Harris, who was the Deputy Headmaster at Cropwell Manor Private School, plus Bill's secretary and some of his regular workmen, plumbers, carpenters, tilers, bricklayers and painters and decorators - all those who had helped Bill, in their spare time, to renovate the house along with their wives or girlfriends. The house was soon full of laughter and chatter.

They all had a wonderful evening, and Claudia smiled when she saw her sister looking happy and radiant in the company of Bill's cousin, Simon. Simon was as tall as Bill, but much slimmer. His brown hair was wavy and his grey eyes were warm behind rimless glasses as they gazed at Colette.

"How do I tell the difference between you and your sister?" he had asked her when they were introduced.

"Easy!" laughed Colette. "I'm the bossy one!"

The party went on until late, and they all slept in the next morning. Bill then looked after Lucy whilst the women cleaned up after breakfast and prepared Sunday lunch.

Much to Colette's delight, Simon had been invited to dinner, and when he arrived he made a beeline for her. Bill nudged Claudia.

"Seen those two?"

"Yes, I have. Do you think it's love at first sight?" she whispered.

"It certainly looks like it." "I think it's wonderful," beamed Claudia.

The weeks sped by and Claudia and Lucy were happy in their new home. Colette made her usual visits, but spent a lot of time with Simon. Maureen would often baby-sit so that the four of them could have a night out. Claudia always felt so much happier when she was with her twin.

As Christmas drew near, Claudia smiled at Bill.

"You do realise that I tend to get pregnant about this time of year?"

"Well, let's hope you get pregnant this Christmas," grinned Bill, slipping his arms round her.

She did.

When Lucy was told she was going to have a baby brother or sister, she was thrilled, and ran round telling everyone she met. She was even more excited when she was told she was going to have two brothers or sisters, and was soon trotting about with two dolls in her pram instead of one.

"Look, Mummy, I've got twins!" she would shout happily. Claudia's insides turned over.

Bill was overjoyed at the prospect of being a father, but Claudia was still reeling from the shock of hearing she was to have another set of twins! As usual she felt very sick for the first few weeks, so Bill employed a local woman to come in and help with the housework and keep an eye on Lucy. She was a friend of Maureen's called Rose White, a retired nurse who had worked for many years with Maureen. Rose was lonely as her husband had recently died, and her only son was living abroad with his family. Although they had invited Rose to go and live with them she did not want to leave her cottage, which was full of happy memories, and her friends.

Rose was tall and thin with a mop of curly white hair, brown eyes and a well-shaped mouth under a rather beaky nose. She looked rather like a bird - until she smiled, when her face would light up, making her look younger and more attractive.

Rose loved working at Chimneys. She liked Bill and Claudia on sight, and adored little Lucy. Lucy would follow her about and try to help her with household chores, and when she tilted her head to one side to look up at Rose when she asked her a question, Rose could have hugged her.

"What an adorable child!" Rose would think to herself as she busied about.

By the summer the family were settled and happy. Rose fitted well into the household, keeping the house clean and looking after them all. She would arrive in the morning to clean up and look after Lucy, and prepare the dinner before she left. Some days she would even stay and cook it, and refused to take any extra wages.

"Rose, you are so good to us," Claudia would say. "What would we do without you?"

"I'm happy to be here, Claudia, it's good for me to be here with a family - I was getting very lonely."

Bill always gave Rose the weekend off, and then Maureen would pop in to see if she could do anything to help. Lucy was always pleased to see her 'Nan'.

"People have been so kind to me," Claudia would say to Bill. "It's almost as if they know how miserable I was in Italy, but they don't."

Claudia had no idea how frail and nervous she often looked - she unwittingly made people feel that they wanted to take care of her.

Claudia grew large and uncomfortable carrying her twins, and knew, as before that they would be born early. One evening during the summer she and Bill were sitting on the patio in soft armchairs, watching the sun set over the trees.

"Are you alright, love?" asked Bill as he watched Claudia move her hands over her swollen body, a frown creasing her forehead.

"Yes, I'm O.K... but... Bill..."

"What is it?"

"When I've had the twins - if they are both O.K... would you mind if I was sterilised...?"

"Of course not, love. You will have had five children by then - I wouldn't expect you to risk having any more."

"Dear Bill," she smiled, putting her small hand over his large, weatherbeaten one.

A week later Claudia was taken into hospital where she gave birth to another set of identical twin boys. They were called Luke, after Bill's father and Mark, after Claudia's. The two little boys were eight weeks early and spent their early days in incubators.

Bill and Claudia were thrilled with their little sons.

"They've got your blond hair, Claudia."

"Yes, but they look like you, Bill."

Lucy was also delighted with her two baby brothers, and could barely wait for them to be brought home.

While Claudia was in hospital recovering from the birth and her sterilisation, life was hectic at Chimneys. Maureen and Rose were looking after an excited Lucy. Colette and Rachel came to visit on their days off, and Simon made regular visits. Each day someone would take Lucy to the hospital to see Claudia and the twins. Lucy's young life was turned upside down with all the excitement and the constant visitors.

When Claudia and the boys finally arrived home, it was still hectic. There were two crying babies needing to be fed and changed at all hours of the day and night. The house was full of visitors all day, and there were visits from the local midwife and health visitor, who would check and weigh the babies, to save Claudia the hassle of trying to get them to the clinic. There were still visits from Colette, Rachel and Simon, all wanting to help, and Maureen and Rose happily spent their time washing and ironing and cleaning, cooking and making pots of tea.

Lucy adored her little brothers, and was always wanting to touch them and kiss them and hold their tiny hands. She would happily run backwards and forwards, fetching and carrying for her mother, and was rewarded by being allowed to hold a bottle, and carefully feed Mark, then Luke, while they were propped up in Claudia's hands, as they were too small to be held in the crook of her arm.

One day Rose was watching Lucy as she happily pushed her two dolls around in their pram, her dark, shiny ponytail swinging.

"Your Lucy is marvellous, Claudia, she is so family-orientated."

Rose didn't notice the colour drain out of Claudia's face.

Claudia's heart sank. Lucy was just like Attilio's family - whatever would she say if she knew she had two older brothers? Whatever would she say if she knew that her mother had run away and left them? Claudia closed her eyes.

"Dear God," she prayed,"please don't let her ever find out!"

SEVEN

LUCY 1977-1984

Lucy was growing up a happy but excitable child who adored her little brothers.

As Mark and Luke grew a little bigger, Claudia decided to join the Twins Club, and with the help of Maureen, they would go once a week, where Claudia had a chance to meet other mothers who had twins. Lucy was very protective of her little brothers, and would hold on to the twin buggy like a watchdog, chatting away to them and proudly showing them off to everyone.

"Mummy, does everybody have twins?" she asked frowning, when she realised just how many sets of twins were at the club every week.

"No, darling," laughed Claudia, "not everybody."

"I want twins when I grow up," Lucy stated firmly.

Claudia stroked her daughter's dark, silky hair and smiled.

"There's every chance that you might, Lucy."

Although Claudia had plenty of help from Rose and Maureen, she was kept so busy she hardly had time to think about the past. Even though she rarely read a newspaper and avoided watching the news on the T.V. she sometimes couldn't avoid seeing Attilio or hearing him sing. Times like this would leave her a nervous wreck for days. She would go unusually quiet and would sneak off for a stiff drink and a couple of cigarettes whenever she had the chance, leaving the children with Rose or Maureen.

One day Claudia's life took a turn for the worse. It was in the August of 1978. Lucy was nearly six years old, and the twins just turned one. It was a lovely summer day, and Claudia and Maureen were taking the twins to the clinic for their injections. Lucy was just recovering from a bout of chicken-pox, so she was going to stay at home with Rose. As it was such a beautiful day Claudia and Maureen had decided to have a walk round Cropwell and do some shopping, after going to the clinic.

When they had gone Rose settled herself on the settee in front of the T.V. and Lucy climbed onto her lap, one arm round her two dolls and a thumb in her mouth, a finger tucked over her nose.

"What would you like on the telly, Lucy?"

"Don't know," came the muffled reply.

Rose flicked over the programmes until she found something she liked. It was a musical, West Side Story, which she loved. She settled down to watch it, her arms round Lucy, and a gentle breeze from the open window ruffled their hair.

Lucy, her eyes closed, lay against Rose, her head tucked under the woman's chin.

The film started off with the two rival gangs dancing across the stage to the lively music. Lucy began to stir. She turned, opened her eyes and watched, her thumb slowly sliding out of her mouth. She watched fascinated, and by the time the lovely song, "Maria", was being sung, Lucy was sitting bold upright on Rose's lap.

Rose watched in amazement as Lucy absorbed the film, trying to join in the singing and bobbing up and down on Rose's knee to the lively songs. Lucy was enthralled.

Just as the film finished, Claudia and Maureen walked in carrying the twins. Lucy jumped off Rose's lap and ran to her mother, her eyes bright and happy.

"Mummy, mummy," she cried. "We've had on the lovely music, and it made me feel all funny inside!"

"What!" gasped Claudia, staring at Rose. "What does she mean?"

Rose looked up and smiled. "We've just watched 'West Side Story' and Lucy loved it. I didn't realise she could sing." Claudia paled. "She's quite amazing," continued Rose. "It's such a grown-up sort of film for a little girl to love."

Claudia felt ill - it was as if her worst nightmare was coming true.

Lucy began dancing and singing round the room.

"Lucy, be quiet!" Claudia snapped.

Rose and Maureen looked at each other and frowned. Maureen broke up the tense atmosphere.

"Come on, Lucy, come and watch the twins while we get them some tea."

Lucy put down her dolls and moved towards her baby brothers who had started to crawl about. She glared at her mother - her mouth turning down at the corners. She tossed her head and Claudia froze.

"Oh, no," she thought to herself," she looks just like Isabella having a sulk - please, God no!"

"Are you alright, Claudia?" Rose asked, puzzled.

"Oh, yes, I'm fine, thanks."

The rest of the afternoon passed in a haze. Lucy stormed off in a sulk while the three women sorted out the shopping and the twins.

When Bill came home shortly afterwards, he found Rose and Maureen in the living room feeding the twins, who were sitting in their high-chairs kicking their feet in unison, Lucy out of sight, and Claudia in the kitchen smoking a cigarette with trembling fingers.

"What's wrong?" he asked quietly.

"N...nothing."

"Claudia..."

"I'll tell you later."

At that moment Lucy came running in, arms outstretched.

"Daddy!"

"Hello, sweetheart." Bill picked her up and she flung her arms round his neck and buried her face in his shoulder.

"You alright, Lucy?"

"Mummy shouted at me!"

Bill frowned and looked at Claudia.

"What has she done?"

"Nothing," was the hushed reply. She pointed to the living room where Maureen and Rose were feeding the twins.

Bill knew he would have to wait.

The house was quiet. Bill was upstairs tucking Lucy into bed - the twins were already asleep. Claudia was in the kitchen preparing some salad for their tea.

Bill walked into the kitchen.

"Claudia, what's wrong?" He put his hands on her shoulders and gently turned her round to face him. She wiped away tears with the backs of her hands.

"Tell me what's wrong," he urged.

With a sniff, Claudia told him, haltingly, what had happened.

"Oh, come on Claudia. All little girls like to sing, it's only natural, and she's bound to sulk at times, and she's also bound to look a little bit like Isabella, after all, the woman is her aunt."

"Bill, I don't want her to sing. I don't want her to grow up and be a singer. I don't want her ever to meet her father. If he finds me he might have me killed."

Bill squeezed her shoulders. "Claudia, there is no guarantee that she will turn out to be a singer. It's not as if her father is even famous. I've never heard of a singer called Attilio Rossini."

"He... he's changed his name," she stammered.

"Well, what does he call himself now?"

Claudia took a deep breath and looked up at Bill with wide, frightened eyes.

"He... he's... changed it to... T... Tony Ross."

There was a tense silence as Bill stared at her in total disbelief.

"Tony Ross. *THE* Tony Ross! Claudia, you've got to be kidding me!"

"No, no, it's true."

"But he's become one of the most famous singers in the world!"

"I know."

"How can you be sure?"

"I've seen him on the T.V."

Bill let go of Claudia and ran his big hands through his thick hair, as he began pacing the kitchen.

"Tony Ross," he mumbled."Tony bloody Ross!" He came back to face her. "Why didn't you tell me?"

"I didn't think it was fair for you to see him on the T.V. and in the papers and know he was my husband." She started to cry again. Bill pulled her into his arms and stroked her hair. He closed his eyes to try and shut out the face of Tony Ross, which was filling his head.

Eventually he spoke. "Don't worry, love, I understand, and I promise I'll try my best to discourage Lucy from going into showbusiness - if that's what she wants."

"I could do with a drink," sniffed Claudia.

"So could I. Come on." Bill led her into the living room and got them both a whisky. They sat on the settee and Claudia groped for a cigarette with trembling hands. Bill sat in silence trying to absorb the shock - a shock which had hit him like a bolt out of the blue.

In the September of that year, Lucy was in her second year at school. She loved being with other children and would mother all the smaller ones. It was as school that Lucy met her lifelong friend Rebecca Lawson, usually known as Becky or Bex. Becky was a very pretty girl with fair hair tied up in long, fluffy bunches, and big blue eyes. She lived in a modest three-bedroomed house on the edge of town, with an older sister and their parents.

Lucy and Becky became inseparable, mainly because they both liked music, and they would sing lustily at every opportunity. Although Lucy was well-behaved at school, she became moody and sulky at home, as every time she burst into song

Claudia would send her up to her room, saying her singing gave her a headache.

Although Claudia was frantic about Lucy wanting to sing, it didn't stop her from having some happy moments with her family. Some evenings they would all sit on the settee together to watch something on the T.V. Lucy on Bill's knee, and the twins on Claudia's. Lucy would look adoringly at her little brothers and try to hold their small hands in her own.

As Mark and Luke, got bigger the three of them would play wildly together, chasing each other through the house, running up the stairs in the kitchen, dashing along the landing, and racing down the other flight of stairs into the dining room. On wet days they would play hide-and-seek in the large, rambling house, and on summer days the three of them would run, squealing, through the tall shrubbery, which hid their small bodies, then run down to the wrought iron railing at the bottom of the garden, and peer down into the water rushing below. Lucy would often tell them scary stories, and they would gaze at her, spellbound.

When Claudia watched Lucy with her little brothers, she always felt guilty.

"What would Lucy say if she knew about Claudy and Tilly?" she thought. "She would never forgive me!"

Although her love for Attilio had faded over the years, she was still acutely aware of him whenever he appeared on the T.V. unexpectedly. Her inside would churn when she saw him being interviewed or at an awards ceremony with a beautiful woman on his arm. Bill would grip her hand, knowing the guilt she was going through.

When Lucy was eight years old Colette and Simon got married. Lucy revelled in all the excitement. She was to be a bridesmaid to her aunt, and the twins page-boys, dressed in navy blue velvet suits with fluffy white shirts. Lucy looked like a dream in a long navy dress and shoes. Her dark hair had been piled on top of her head in curls, with a spray of blue flowers winding through, and long blue ribbons hanging down the back. She carried a spray of blue and white flowers.

Colette, as expected, looked stunning in a long white elegant dress. Her swept up hair boasted a tiara and a short, fluffy veil which floated down to her waist.

The wedding took place in the tiny church opposite Chimneys. The small church was soon filled. Lucy loved the singing and her young voice floated sweetly above everyone else's. The reception was held at the nearby White Horse. It was a happy day for everyone.

Colette gave up her job and moved into Cropwell to be with her new husband.

Two years later she gave birth to a son, Martin, to Claudia's delight. Colette was now a full-time housewife and mother - much to Claudia's relief.

EIGHT

PROBLEMS 1985 – 1994

Over the years, Lucy and Claudia slowly grew apart. Life was an ongoing battle between them, Lucy wanting to sing and her mother saying 'no'. There were constant tantrums and rows and Lucy grew more and more like Isabella with her sulks. Claudia's patience grew thin.

In the September of 1990, Lucy and Becky, both now 12 years old, started at Cropwell Manor Grammar School. The two attractive girls settled in well, and it didn't take long for pupils and teachers to discover Lucy's talent as a singer. A lot of the children were in awe of her. She was so beautiful and talented, others were jealous and spiteful, but Lucy would merely glare at them and then toss her head in disdain, one hand sweeping her hair it over her shoulder.

One day she came home from school in a towering rage. Bill and Claudia were startled.

"What's up, Lucy?" asked Bill.

"What's up?" she yelled. "I'll tell you what's up! People at school are saying that I'm adopted, and that you're not my real parents!"

"Adopted! What on earth are you talking about?" snapped Claudia angrily.

"Lucy, calm down and explain." Bill's voice was firm.

"Some people say that I look nothing like you or Mum, or the twins. They say I'm different!"

Bill was angry. "Lucy, that is total rubbish! I was with your mother when you born, and I never want to hear you say that again! Now apologise!"

Lucy glared at her mother sulkily. "I'm sorry." Then she turned on her heel and stormed off to the bedroom. Claudia looked up at Bill.

"What are we going to do with her?"

"She's at a difficult age, Claudia."

"Difficult? She's a nightmare!"

Although Lucy was difficult at home, she had become popular at school now. She wasn't over keen on schoolwork, but loved her music lessons. At the end of the lesson, Joyce Davis, her teacher would make the class sit quietly and listen to some classical music. As the music began to play, Lucy would feel herself begin to float on air, as if her whole body was being transported on a wave of emotion. Music was in her blood.

Lucy was given plenty of encouragement by her teachers, particularly Joyce Davis and her English teacher, Henry Kendal, who were totally puzzled by her mother's attitude. On her behalf, Henry Kendal spoke to Claudia on an open day when parents were invited to meet their children's teachers. He was shocked by Claudia's frozen look and angry comments.

While her children were at school Claudia spent time with her sister - the one person she could really share her troubles with. She was also glad of the company of Maureen and Rose who were now in their seventies. Maureen had grown rather plump, and her sense of humour always managed to cheer Claudia up. They would often meet for lunch in Cropwell. Rose, who was looking more bird-like than ever, was still cleaning the house for Claudia, her thin body still full of energy.

Although Lucy was unhappy at home battling with her mother, she still loved her young brothers, and even though they were getting more grown up, they still liked their lovely big sister to sneak into their room at night, tell them stories, and sing them softly to sleep.

Sometimes Lucy would be in despair. Her mother, who she was now growing to hate, still would not let her sing in the house or play music. Her brothers were only interested in beastly football, and although her father was always kind and generous he didn't know anything about music. Her Aunt Colette was not much better, either. She always supported her mother - being identical twins, they were very close.

Lucy started spending more time at the home of her friend, Becky, whose parents would let the girls sing and play music as much as they wished.

One day at school, Lucy was approached by her music teacher, Joyce Davis. It was the spring of 1988 and Lucy was 14.

"Lucy, do you want to become a professional singer?"

"Oh, yes, Mrs Davis, I do."

"Good. Now Lucy, if you want to do this, your voice will have to trained."

"Trained?"

"Oh, yes. Trained properly, and I have a suggestion to make. I'm prepared to spend half an hour of every day of my own lunch hour to train you. Would you like that?"

"Oh, Mrs Davis, yes please! That would be wonderful!"

"Right, now I want you to meet me in the Music Room each day at 12.30, OK?"

"Oh, yes, cried Lucy again, "and thank you!"

Joyce Davis was a popular teacher. Average height and slightly plump, she had a round, pretty face, wore horn-rimmed glasses and her short, wavy brown hair tended to look rather wild as she constantly ran her hands through it. She favoured long, floaty skirts and clumpy shoes.

The following day, Lucy started her singing lessons.

Every year Cropwell Grammar School would put on a school play or a musical. It would be performed for three nights in the school hall, and pupils' family and friends were all invited.

During her years at school, Lucy always took the lead in the musicals. Everyone thought she was marvellous – but her parents never went to see her.

Although Cropwell was only a small market town, it was gradually expanding, and one day the New Cropwell Theatre was opened. The theatre was mainly for amateurs and was extremely popular. The theatre was built in the city centre. Downstairs, on the ground floor were the theatre box-office, dressing rooms and workshop for making and storing scenery, and a bar which was only opened during performances. There was also a trendy wine bar that sold light meals and drinks. This was open all day to members of the public, and was also very popular.

Upstairs were the offices and the Green Room (an actor's bar) and the rehearsal room for the Cropwell Operatic Society, the Cropwell Drama Group and the Cropwell Dancing School. They all rehearsed on different nights so that members could be in more than one group at a time. Each society put on two shows a year and at Christmas all three would join up together to put on a spectacular show.

Joyce Davis was one of the people in the charge of the Operatic Society, and her husband and son both played in the orchestra. One day she suggested that Lucy and Becky, should join it. Becky had no problems, but Lucy knew she was going to have trouble.

She went home to Chimneys in a belligerent mood. With sinking heart Claudia saw her daughter, now looking very grown up, arrive home looking as sulky as Isabella at her worst!

When Bill arrived home he saw Claudia frowning.

"What's up?"

"Lucy looks in an evil mood."

Bill rubbed his big hands through his hair. "I wonder what she wants?"

They were soon to find out.

Lucy stormed into the kitchen. Bill looked up. "What is it, Lucy?"

Lucy glared at her parents, hands on her hips. "I want to join the Cropwell Theatre, so that I can sing."

Claudia's face drained of colour. "No, Lucy!"

"Why not?"

"You're not going to be a singer, I won't allow it!"

Lucy's eyes blazed as she glared at her mother.

"You hate me! There can't be any other reason why you won't ler me sing! Well, I hate you too, and when I'm old enough I'm going to run away from here and become a singer whether you like it or not. I hate you!" She then turned and, sobbing, flew upstairs to her room and threw herself on her bed, beating the pillow with her fists.

By the time Lucy had got upstairs, Claudia was also in floods of tears.

"Bill, what am I going to do?" she wept. Bill took her in his arms and stroked her blonde hair. "Bill, I can't let her become a singer. She might meet Attilio, he might guess who she is..."

"Claudia, don't..."

"She's going to run away..."

Bill gripped her firmly by the shoulders and looked down into her stricken face. "Claudia, we'll have to compromise."

"C... compromise... how?"

"Let her go."

"No! No!"

"Claudia, listen to me. Cropwell Theatre is for amateurs. We'll tell her she can go, as long as she doesn't turn professional. If she promises, it'll be all O.K."

Claudia clutched at Bill's sweater. "Bill, it's not just Attilio..."

"What do you mean?"

"It's Claudy and Tilly."

"What about them?"

"They're singing now, too. They were on the front of the newspaper the other day when I went into town. I bought a copy...it's upstairs."

"Bloody Hell!"

"They call themselves the Denver Brothers"

"The Denver Brothers?"

"Yes. Claudy is called Clay and Tilly is called Leo."

"Oh, God, that's all we need!"

"I know," Claudia replied faintly.

"Well, are we agreed on Lucy?"

"Yes... O.K"

"Good girl! Now you come and sit down, and I'll go and talk to her." Bill settled the trembling Claudia in an armchair and, leaving her with a brandy and a cigarette, he made his way upstairs and tapped on Lucy's door.

"Lucy, it's me, Dad. I'm coming in." He gently opened the door, let himself in, and eased his large body onto the edge of her bed.

"It's O.K. Lucy, you can go."

Lucy turned her tear-stained face towards him.

"Oh, Dad!" she cried, and threw herself into his arms. He hugged her tightly, and laid his cheek against her dark, shining head.

"There are conditions, Lucy."

She lifted her head and looked at him with dark, watery eyes. He spoke gently to her.

"Lucy, I'll give you everything you need if you want to join the Cropwell Theatre. You can have money for make-up and costumes or whatever, but you must promise me that you won't go professional."

"But why?"

"Because showbusiness is a very dodgy life - you could be in and out of work and meet constant disappointment. It's better for you to be the best singer in Cropwell than perhaps a second-rate or out-of-work singer in the big, bad world. You do understand?"

"Yes, O.K. Dad."

"And by the way, your mother doesn't hate you, she loves you very much. She's just afraid of losing you. You O.K. now?"

Lucy looked up at Bill with eyes that would melt an iceberg.

"Daddy, I do love you so," she said softly, slipping her arms round Bill's neck.

"And I love you too, sweetheart." Bill wrapped his big arms round Lucy. He closed his eyes and prayed. "Please, God, don't ever let her find out that I'm not her father!"

So Lucy and Becky joined the Cropwell Operatic Society and the Cropwell Dancing School the following week, and enjoyed every minute of it. Lucy changed her name to Lucilla Lane, and young though she was she was soon taking the leading roles, her voice growing richer, stronger and more powerful. Becky was quite happy to take more minor roles, knowing her voice would never be as good as her friend's.

During the years that followed, Lucy was totally happy. Her whole being came alive when she sang and she felt as if she was floating on air. She worked relentlessly on all her parts, such as Eliza Doolittle in "My Fair Lady" - Eva Peron in "Evita" and Anna in the "King and I".

When Lucy and Becky had reached 16 they had both left school. As they were both artistic, they had decided to become hairdressers. Their training had included two years at the local college with a day release at a hairdressing salon. Becky also took on a make-up and beauty course. She told Lucy, "When you're famous, Lucy, I shall be you personal make-up artist and hairdresser!"

"Thanks, Bex!" Lucy had laughed.

Once Lucy and Becky had finished their training they both got jobs in Cropwell, Lucy in the hairdressing department of a large department store, and Becky in a high-class salon. The two girls passed their driving tests when they were 17, and Bill bought Lucy a white mini for her 18th birthday, while Becky's father bought her a second-hand Fiesta. The two girls would take it in turns to pick each other up for work.

Now they were both working girls, they would go shopping together, and go to London to see some of the wonderful shows - "Phantom of the Opera" left Lucy on a cloud for days. On a Saturday night the two of them would go to a nightclub, where they would dance the night away, feet tapping, heads bobbing and hair flying.

Lucy was having a wonderful life.

She told her mother - nothing.

In the September of 1994, when Lucy had just turned 21, Bill was down at Gage's Farm, as the farmer wanted an estimate for some work. While he was there, the farmer's wife brought him out a cup of tea.

"Hello there, Bill. How are you?"

"Fine, thanks, and you?"

"I'm fine," she paused. "Bill, I must just say how wonderful your daughter is."

"Oh, thank you."

"You must be very proud of her."

"Yes, of course."

"I saw her last night at the Cropwell Theatre. She was playing Maria in West Side Story. It was the best performance I've ever seen. Have you seen it yet?"

"Er... not yet," mumbled Bill. He left the farm feeling guilty.

The farmer and his wife looked at each other.

"His wife is a miserable bugger!"

"I know. A lot of people don't like her. She won't let young Lucy be a professional, you know. And it's such a shame - she's brilliant."

"So I hear - they never go and watch her."

"I know. That's why I asked Bill if he'd seen her in West Side Story. I know it wasn't very nice of me, but I couldn't help it."

"Bill's a good chap. It's 'er that's the miserable one."

When Bill got into his Landrover, he was frowning. He did feel guilty about never seeing Lucy perform - but he hadn't wanted to upset Claudia. Yet he could watch Lucy without his wife knowing - couldn't he? Before he could change his mind he drove into Cropwell, parked the car and went to the theatre box-office to see if he could get a ticket. They had one for the following night - a middle seat at the back of the stalls. Bill bought the ticket and put it in his wallet.

The following night Bill told Claudia he was going to a meeting and set off wearing a suit and tie. Claudia was quite happy to sit curled up on the settee with a drink and a cigarette, watching "Eastenders" and "Coronation Street" until Mark and Luke came in from the gym and plonked themselves beside her, before persuading her to get them another meal, as they were always hungry.

Mark and Luke were now 6-foot teenagers, both with a mass of blond hair like Claudia and bodies like Bill. They were like two giants - and they adored their mother.

Bill drove nervously into Cropwell. He had never been in a theatre in his life and was feeling uneasy. After parking the car in the car park at the back of the theatre, he followed a crowd of people into the building. He bought a programme and handed his ticket to a lady at the door of the auditorium, who showed him where to sit. Settling comfortably into his seat, he looked round. The theatre was almost full, and there was a buzz of conversation. The seats were all covered in a soft red material, as was the large curtain hanging at the front of the stage. There were four boxes on each side of the auditorium, and they were all full. More people came in and started making their way along the rows.

Bill looked down at the programme and searched the cast list looking for Lucy's name. His heart missed a beat - it wasn't there! He frantically turned the pages to find some photos of the cast - and there she was! He looked underneath the photo and there was the name Lucilla Lane. Bill sighed with relief that he had found her picture and that she had changed her name.

Suddenly the lights began to fade and the orchestra started to play the overture. Bill could feel the tension in the atmosphere as the audience waited. He heard a woman whisper beside him.

"I've only come to see Lucilla Lane - she's marvellous!"

"I know - she's going to be famous one day."

"I got her autograph on my last programme," whispered her companion.

Suddenly the music changed and the curtain slowly lifted and disappeared. Two rival gangs of youths began dancing across the stage, whistling and clicking their fingers. They were the Jets and the Sharks, one gang being American and the other the

Puerto Rican. Bill watched, frowning, this certainly was not his cup of tea! He waited patiently to see Lucy.

His heart missed a beat when he saw her. She was in a dress shop wearing a white dress with a red belt, her dark hair swept back behind her ears. She looked so young and innocent, and when she began to sing she took his breath away.

He watched the rest of the show in a daze. He listened to Lucy sing the lovely song "Tonight" with the hero, Tony, and enjoyed the lively song "America."

When the safety curtain came down for the interval, Bill sat in his seat, unable to move. People got up and moved away from either side of him to go to the bar or get ice-creams, but he was rooted to the spot. He would have loved a drink, but he was in such a state of shock his legs would not carry him.

After a 15-minute interval, the second half of the show began. Bill sat mesmorised as he watched Lucy. The show was similar to Claudia's past - the girl, Maria, falling in love with the American Tony, the two families hating each other - it was very emotional. He sat and smiled when Lucy sang the lovely song "I feel pretty" as she danced round the stage, her body graceful, her eyes shining. He also liked the mock wedding between Maria and Tony, and the song with the words "one life" and "a time and place for us" brought tears to his eyes. The story became exciting when the two gangs began fighting and Tony finally killed Maria's brother, Bernado. Bill grew tense when Lucy, as Maria, found her lover dead, and sank to the floor singing the heartbreaking words "hold my hand... I'll take you there..."

As the musical finished, there was a storm of applause. Bill was caught up in the atmosphere and applauded along with everyone else. There were shouts and wolf-whistles as Lucy came forward to bow to the audience - people started to stand and cheer as the curtain slid up and down for further curtain calls.

Feeling embarrassed at the emotion that had welled up inside, Bill hurried out of the theatre, pushing past the crowds.

He got to his car, climbed in and then sat with his elbows on the steering wheel, his head buried in his hands.

What was he going to do?

He loved Claudia and understood her fears about Lucy ever meeting her real father and brothers.

But he also loved Lucy and her performance tonight had been out of this world. She was talented and brilliant and he was having to hold her back. What was he going to do?

Bill Harris was being torn apart.

NINE

MYSTERY 1994

At 21 Lucy and Becky had the world at their feet. They were both attractive and talented, had steady jobs, their own cars and plenty of boyfriends.

Lucy was disdainful of most boys, saying they were silly and immature. The only man she really liked was Ricky Knight, who always played opposite her as leading man. He was a local lawyer and a brilliant singer - slightly taller than Lucy with thick straight blond hair and greeny-blue eyes. Unfortunately he was engaged to another girl, and although Lucy would never have tried to take him away from his fiancée, she certainly made the most of it when playing romantic parts with him on stage!

Lucy enjoyed her job at the hairdressers and most of her clients had seen her performing at the Cropwell Theatre.

One Saturday when Lucy was working, one of her regular customers, Mrs. Jackson, came in to have a cut and blow-dry. They were chatting while Lucy was expertly snipping away at the curly locks.

"Lucy, I saw you last night playing Mrs. Johnstone in 'Blood Brothers'. You really were wonderful, dear, I think everyone in the audience was crying at the end."

"Thank you, Mrs. Jackson," laughed Lucy happily.

"Who do you take after?"

"Take after?"

"Well, someone in your family must be a singer. A talent like yours is always hereditary."

"I don't know," replied Lucy, frowning.

"Do your parents sing at all?"

"No."

"What about your grandparents?"

"I don't know. My mother's parents were killed in an avalanche before I was born, and my dad's parents died long ago."

"Well, Lucy, you really should trace your ancestors. I can guarantee that somewhere along the line you'll find a singer."

Lucy was thoughtful. "How would I start doing that?"

"To start off with, you need to collect all the certificates you can get. You can start with your own birth certificate. This gives you the names of your parents and your father's occupation. You then get hold of your parents' marriage certificate, as this will give you the names and occupations of *their* fathers. After that you get your parents' birth certificates, which will give you your grandparents' names and your grandfathers' occupations. You just keep going back getting births and marriages. Give it a try and if you get stuck I can always help you."

"Have you traced your family tree, Mrs. Jackson?"

"Oh, yes. I've been doing it for years. It's the most exciting hobby I've ever had. You never know what you're going to turn up!" she grinned wickedly.

"Where would I get certificates from?" asked Lucy, who was now growing really interested.

"Your parents will already have some in the house, I expect, so check those first. You don't want to go paying £6.50 for a certificate unnecessarily. Now, if your parents come from round here you can go to the local registry office and get them, but they won't do a lengthy search, so you would have to have a pretty good idea of the year you're looking for. If you don't want to do that you can go to the Cropwell Library, as they have the entries from the General Registry Office on microfiche, then you can send off to the General Register Office in London or Southport. You can also go the the Leicestershire Record Office in Wigston and check the church records for baptisms, marriages and burials, and get photocopies."

"Gracious!" exclaimed Lucy. "That's a lot of places!"

Mrs. Jackson chuckled. "That's nothing, Lucy. There are endless more sources for tracing your ancestors. What I've told you is just the beginning!"

By the time Lucy had finished work, she was in a state of excitement about the possibility of finding a singer in her past. When she met Becky she told her about it.

"That's a good idea," replied Becky. "When are you going to start?"

"Tonight," replied Lucy firmly.

Becky laughed. "Trust you, Lucy. You can't wait a minute!"

"I know I'm impatient, Bex, I just can't help it!"

"Are you going to tell your mum and dad?"

"No fear! You know what Mum's like - she's scared of everything and everybody. She'd only try and put me off."

"That's true, but how can you go rummaging through your parents' things without them knowing?"

"Easy," laughed Lucy. "They'll be out. Mum and Dad are going to a do and the twins always go out on a Saturday night."

"Would you like me to help you look?"

"Oh, yes please! If you come round for me at about 7.30, Mum and Dad will just be going out. As soon as they've gone we'll nip up to their room and have a nosey and then we'll go on to that new night-club and meet up with the others."

"Good idea," replied Becky with a grin.

At 7.30 that night Lucy was dressed ready to go out in silky black trousers, a white top dashed with silver, and black clumpy shoes. Becky arrived just as Claudia and Bill were leaving.

Claudia did not look happy. She hardly ever saw her daughter, who was out at work all day, out every night, either at the Cropwell Theatre or at Becky's.

"Gosh, Lucy, your mum looks more miserable than ever!"

"I know," replied Lucy scornfully. "We hardly ever speak!"

When they heard Bill and Claudia drive away, the two girls crept upstairs to their bedroom. Lucy pulled open a wardrobe door and opened a drawer.

"They keep all their papers and stuff in here," whispered Lucy. She rummaged through and brought out a manilla folder with the word 'certificates' scrawled across the front. "Here we are!" she cried. The two girls sat on the floor and Lucy eased the documents out of the folder. Heads together, they began reading.

"These are Mark's and Luke's, see - father William Morris, a builder and Claudia Harris, formerly Morris."

"Why have they got times on?"

"Because they're twins - I suppose they have to know which one was born first, because he would be the eldest, even if it was only by a few minutes. Look, here's Mum's - it's the same, see, because she's a twin."

"Oh, yes. I see she was born in Borehamwood - that's London, isn't it?"

"Yes, the outskirts, and look - her parents were Mark Morris and Lucy Ann Morris, formerly Forrester."

"She wasn't a singer, was she?"

"I don't think so. Look here's Dad's - he was born in Cropwell - father Luke Harris, a builder, and Jane Harris, formerly King."

"Still no singer, Lucy."

"No… oh...no!"

"What's up?"

"This is my birth certificate...it's only a short one - would you believe it!"

"Let me see." Lucy passed the birth certificate to Becky, who frowned.

"Lucy, what does this say?"

Lucy looked at it again. "It says Lucy Harris, born 15th September, 1973 - registered in Cropwell."

"Lucy, look at it again," said Becky quietly. Lucy looked at it again, her brow wrinkled.

"What's wrong with it?"

Becky took a deep breath. "It doesn't say Lucy Harris - it says Lucy Morris."

"What!" Lucy stared at her birth certificate in amazement. "I don't believe it!" she cried. "I must be illegitimate." Her face drained of colour.

"Perhaps your real dad was a singer," suggested Becky, but Lucy just stared at her friend, her eyes filling with tears.

"But that means Dad isn't my dad!" she cried.

"I'm sorry, Lucy," mumbled Becky.

"I can' believe it...I just can't believe it! I can't ever remember being without Dad. He's always been here. I've even got photos of him holding me as a baby."

"Perhaps he is your dad. He may have married your mum after you were born."

"But he was with Mum when I was born, he told me himself."

"Why would he say that?"

"Because I told him I thought I was adopted, because the kids at school said I looked different from the rest of my family. He was furious. I'm sure I told you about it."

"Is their marriage certificate here?" suggested Becky. Lucy searched through the certificates again, and shook the folder.

"It's not here!"

"Are you sure?"

"Yes. God, this is getting worse!"

"Well, it looks as if they were married when they had Mark and Luke."

"Yes, it does."

"Maybe your mum had a boyfriend who ditched her when she got pregnant, and your dad married her later," suggested Becky.

"I suppose so, but I can't imagine my mum being in that position - she's such a scaredy cat and so prim and proper."

"Perhaps your dad was married to somebody else?"

"He was, but she died before he met Mum."

"Are you sure?"

"Why?"

"She could have run off and left him, and he could have told your mum she'd died."

"I suppose it's possible - but I can't believe he would do that. Becky, if he's not my dad, why didn't he tell me?"

"He adores you, Lucy, you're the apple of his eye. He probably wouldn't want you to know."

"Becky, I'm so shocked, I feel sick."

Becky, always the calmer of the two, put an arm round her friend's shoulder.

"Come on, Lucy, let's put these away and go downstairs, and I'll get you a brandy."

"O.K. but let's just check these other folders in case their marriage certificate is in another one."

They both searched, but all they found were mortgage, car and insurance policies.

The two girls made their way downstairs, and sat on the settee. Becky got them both a brandy. Lucy looked forlornly at her friend.

"How could they have kept a secret like this from me all these years?"

"People do, Lucy."

"It's no wonder I don't look like my family, if I've got a different father."

"It makes sense, Lucy. Your real father was probably dark like you, and he could have been a singer."

"You're right, Becky."

"Couldn't you get a full birth certificate from somewhere?"

"Of course!" cried Lucy, and told Becky all that Mrs. Jackson had told her.

"We don't want to go to the Cropwell Registry Office - we might know someone in there and they might mention it to your mum and dad."

"Of course. Becky...we could go to London. We'll go on Monday, on our day off!"

"Brilliant idea. I'll find out where it is and we'll go."

The two girls spent the evening chatting about all the possibilities of Lucy's real father. The nightclub was forgotten.

On the Monday morning, Lucy and Becky set off for a day in London. Lucy's insides had been churning non-stop since the awful discovery that she had another father. On the Sunday Becky had made some phone calls.

"We have to go to a place called St. Catherine's House, in a place called Kingsway," she told Lucy. "We have to get a tube to Holborn or we can get a taxi - it's not too far from Euston."

The girls were going to get a cheap day return ticket. Bill slipped some money into Lucy's hand before she left.

"Here you are, sweetheart, treat yourself to something."

"Thanks, Dad." Lucy hugged Bill, fighting back the tears.

Becky picked up Lucy at Chimneys. She was a much better driver than Lucy, calmer, more relaxed and far more capable.

Lucy was in such a tizz that Becky wouldn't risk her life by letting Lucy drive.

They parked Becky's car at Cropwell station, bought their tickets, and were soon racing through the countryside to London. Although the girls had been to London on coach trips to see shows, they had never been round the shops. They decided to visit St. Catherine's House first, and then go shopping.

Lucy decided to use some of Bill's money for taxis, so on getting off the train they dashed through Euston station and down the stairs to the taxi rank. By the time they reached St. Catherine's House it was nearly lunchtime.

They paid the taxi and made their way through the glass revolving doors, then up to a desk to get their bags searched.

"Crikey!" gasped Becky looking round, "this place is packed!"

Ahead of them were hoards of people with note-pads and pens hastily pulling out huge ledgers from metal cabinets, then shoving them back seconds later, and yanking down another one. Everyone was pushing and shoving.

"I didn't expect it to be like this," said Lucy in surprise. "There must be hundreds of people in here."

"What shall we do first?"

"Let's ask at that desk."

They went up to another desk to ask what to do. The lady behind the desk was very helpful. Pointing, she said to them, "All those registers in red are births, those in black are deaths, and the marriages, which are green, are right at the other end. Each year is divided into quarters - March, June, September and December. You'll get a name, a place of registration and a reference number – you'll need all these details when you fill in your order form. All the cabinets have the years printed on the end."

"Thank you very much," said Lucy politely.

They made their way towards the birth section.

"Right," said Becky "we want 1973, the September quarter."

They pushed their way through the milling crowd until they reached the section containing the ledger they wanted.

"You grab a place, Lucy, while I get the ledger down."

Lucy found a space at the edge of the facing counter, while Becky staggered after her with a large, heavy book. Eagerly they turned the pages of lists of typewritten names, until they came to the Ms.

"Gosh, there's a lot of people called Morris!" moaned Lucy, running a finger down the page.

"Here it is!" The girls stared at the entry - Morris - Lucy - Cropwell and a reference number. Becky wrote down the details on a piece of paper in her careful hand.

"Shall we see if we can find your mum and dad's marriage while we're here?"

"Good idea. Come on!"

Lucy and Becky pushed and shoved their way through the crowds and made their way through a door to another large search room at the back of the building.

"We'll start from the time I was born to the time the twins were born," stated Lucy. "That's the September quarter 1973 to the September quarter 1978."

"Right, you grab a place and get the pen and paper, and I'll lug down the books."

"O.K. I'll write M.J.S. and D. at the top and the years down the side, and we can tick off each quarter when we've done it."

Becky got down the first ledger and plonked it on the counter with a thud.

"Right, how do we start marriages?" asked Becky opening up the huge book.

"Need some help?" asked a plump, jolly lady who was standing on the opposite side of the counter.

"Yes, please."

"Both partners' names will be in the book - you have to make sure they both have the same reference number. In these books each person will have their partner's name at the side, but as you get further back it won't."

"How far back do these registers go then?" asked Lucy.

"July, 1837, and those are harder to read because they're still the originals, all written in longhand. The books and pages are thicker and heavier, and you may only get a couple of letters of the alphabet in each one, so you'll get a whole shelf full of registers for just one quarter."

"Thanks for the warning!" smiled Lucy.

The two girls got started. After the first book Lucy stared at Becky.

"I can't believe how many Harrises there are - it's like there are hundreds. There's more of them than the Morrises."

"So I noticed," replied Becky. "You might have had an unusual name, Lucy, it would have been much easier!"

"You mean like - Shufflebottom or Hoo-Flung-Dung?" The girls had a fit of the giggles, then continued searching.

Half and hour later, Becky shut the last ledger, and pushed it back on the shelf.

"Well, it's not here. Are you sure your dad's first wife died?"

"Mmmm...I'm as sure as I can be, I suppose."

"Shall we see if we can find her death?"

"There's not much point - we don't know her first name, and there are so many people called Harris, it would be like looking for a needle in a haystack - and it's so packed in here."

"O.K. then, let's order your birth certificate and get out of here."

They weaved their way through crowds of people, faces alight with excitement as they approached the shelves to start hunting for their elusive ancestors.

Lucy and Becky made their way back to the main search room, picked up a form for a full birth certificate, filled it in carefully and joined the queue to pay for it.

"Look at this flaming queue," grumbled Lucy. "There must be about 50 people in it!"

Becky turned to the lady in front, a tall thin, bird-like lady, who reminded her of Rose.

"Is it always as busy as this?" she asked.

"Oh, yes," smiled the lady. "The best time to come is early in the morning or when there's a tube strike!"

Someone else in the queue started to chuckle and then others joined in the conversation.

"At least these people are all friendly," whispered Lucy to Becky.

The queue moved along quite quickly and the girls soon found themselves at the counter. Lucy handed over the form and the money and the man passed her a brown envelope, telling her to write her name and address on it.

"I can't risk it coming to my house," she whispered frantically to Becky.

"Put my address on then."

"Do we have the same postman?"

"Why?"

"If we do, he might see my name on it, think there's a mistake and shove it through our door."

"O.K. put my name on as well."

Lucy hastily filled out the envelope and handed it back to the man. In return he gave her a receipt and a ticket.

"Make sure you keep this ticket in case you have a query. Your certificate will take about two weeks," he told her.

"Thank you." She turned to Becky. "Two whole weeks!"

They weaved their way out of St. Catherine's House, and found themselves in a busy street, not far from the theatres and Covent Garden.

"Where shall we go?"

"How about Oxford Street? There's lots of shops there."

"O.K."

They hailed a taxi and were soon in Oxford Street.

"Shall we eat first? I'm famished?" said Becky.

"Me too."

"What do you fancy?"

"A hot spicy pizza and a large glass of wine."

"Good idea, come on."

They pushed their way along the crowded street until they found a restaurant. After their meal, they wandered along looking in all the shops.

"London's so crowded!" exclaimed Becky.

"It's wonderful," replied Lucy. "I bet my mum was often in London. I wonder why she left here to go and live in a poky little place like Bishops Fell?"

"She must have had a good reason, I suppose."

The girls had a lovely afternoon going round the shops. They each bought a long denim skirt from a trendy boutique - Lucy's with silver beads and Becky's decorated with embroidery. They also found a large music shop where Lucy bought a tape of classical music conducted by Sir John Phillips, the well-known composer and musician, and Becky bought a tape of the four tenors, Pavarotti, Domingo, Carreras and the fabulous Tony Ross.

Tired after an afternoon of shopping, Lucy and Becky stopped at a Garfunkels restaurant for a steak, salad, chips and wine, and then made their way home.

That night Lucy was so excited thinking about her birth certificate, she hardly slept.

Would it have her real father's name on it or would it simply say: 'father unknown'?

TEN

DISCOVERY 1994/5

Lucy was like a cat on hot bricks during the next two weeks, and Becky looked frantically out of her window every morning for the postman.

It was exactly two weeks later that the brown envelope plopped through Becky's letterbox. She snatched it up and ran to the phone.

"Lucy, it's come!"

"Oh, Becky..."

"I'll pick you up in ten minutes."

"O.K."

It was a beautiful summer morning, but Becky hardly noticed as she drove her car swiftly along the winding country lanes to Chimneys. As soon as she arrived, Lucy came flying out, looking slim and graceful in her pink and white overall and her dark hair scooped up on top of her head to keep her cool.

"Here you are." Becky handed the envelope to Lucy, whose hands were shaking.

Lucy tore open the envelope, her heart pounding. Becky pulled into a lay-by and watched her friend unfold her birth certificate, with her eyes wide and anxious.

"What does it say?"

"There's a name on it!"

"What does it say?"

"It says: father - Attilio Giovanni Rossini, a singer," said Lucy, huskily.

"Blimey... Lucy... a singer! Your Mrs. Jackson was right, you *have* inherited your talent - you've got it from your real father!"

"He sounds like an Italian," murmured Lucy.

"You must take after him in looks, too, Lucy. You do look like an Italian."

"Yes, I do. Becky - how on earth did my mum get mixed up with an Italian singer?"

"She could have met him in a nightclub or something," suggested Becky. "In London you meet people from all over the world all the time."

"Yes, that's true."

"I bet that's why your mum doesn't want you to be a singer - you must remind her of him."

"Either him, or her mistake at getting pregnant."

"No wonder she gets so mad."

"I wonder if he deserted her?"

"He may have been married."

"I can't imagine my mum having an affair with a married man."

"Why not. She's very attractive now. She must have been really beautiful when she was young."

"Yes, of course. You know, Bex, I can hardly believe all this," said Lucy, pointing to the certificate. "A couple of weeks ago I was Lucy Harris, and now I find that my dad's not my dad, my mum had me when she wasn't married, and I'm the illegitimate daughter of some Italian singer I've never heard of! It's all so unbelievable, I don't know whether to laugh or cry."

"What are you going to do, Lucy?"

"I think I'll ask Joyce Davis if she's ever heard of this Attilio Rossini - if not I'll have to wait and try to think about trying to track him down without Mum or Dad knowing."

"It won't be easy - you may have to ask your mum."

"No way – she'd probably have a nervous breakdown! She's such a baby. She has Dad running round, fussing over her and Aunt Colette's always coming to the house mothering her. And she's always telling me off!"

"The thing is, your mum always looks so frail and helpless - she makes people want to look after her."

"Then why didn't this Italian singer look after her?" Lucy demanded hotly."He must have been a right swine - I don't think I will bother to look for him after all."

Nevertheless, after work Lucy and Becky went to see Joyce Davis. They explained Lucy's mystery and showed her the birth certificate.

Joyce frowned. "Well, he certainly has an Italian name, but, no, I've never heard of him. If I do hear anything I'll let you know. And Lucy, I won't tell anyone so don't worry."

The next few weeks flew by, and Lucy's 22nd birthday came and went. She was restless and uneasy and felt she was going to burst inside. She was so full of emotion and longing - she kept feeling she was on the brink of something momentous and exciting, yet she couldn't quite reach it.

How right she was ...

One Thursday night in October, Lucy was hurrying out of work as it was a rehearsal night at the Cropwell Theatre. Lucy and Becky both had good bosses who would always let them go early on their music nights.

As Lucy got outside, she saw Becky waiting for her in the car - waving frantically. She ran to the car and climbed in.

"What's up?"

"Just get in!"

"What's going on?"

"I'll tell you in a minute."

"Why?"

"Because when you see what I've got to show you, you'll either go through the roof of this car, or scream the place down."

"Becky, hurry up and tell me!" Becky drove out onto the Cropwell Road, pulled into a lay-by and stopped the car.

They sat in silence.

"Come on, Becky, what's going on?"

Becky passed Lucy a magazine. "Read this."

Lucy took the magazine and looked down to see an article

on the famous Tony Ross. There was a picture of him looking handsome and smiling. Frowning, Lucy started to read. It was a short article about his career and the careers of his two sons, the Denver Brothers.

"What's this got to do with me?" she asked Becky in a puzzled voice.

"Read to the end," ordered Becky.

Lucy continued to read: 'Although Tony Ross has lived in America for many years he was actually born in Milan in Italy under the name of Attilio Giovani Rossini...'

Lucy sat still, frozen with shock. Becky put a hand on her shoulder and smiled.

"Well, how does it feel to be the daughter of the famous Tony Ross?"

"It...it...can't be true!" whispered Lucy in a choked voice.

"Why not?"

Lucy looked across at her friend, her eyes dark in her now white face. "There's got to be a mistake."

"Why?"

"Why? Because there's no way that my mum could ever have met Tony Ross. It's not possible."

"Has your mum ever been to Italy or America?"

"No...I don't think so...she never goes anywhere."

"But Lucy, we're talking about over 20 years ago. He may not have been famous then."

"But, Becky, look - the Denver Brothers are older than me, Tony Ross was a married man."

"So?"

"I just can't imagine my mum having an affair with a married man."

"Well, she must have gone to bed with him - or in the back of a car," grinned Becky.

"Becky, don't joke!" cried Lucy.

"Perhaps she just had a one-night stand," suggested Becky.

"I can't imagine that, either."

"It does happen, Lucy. And to be honest, if I had the chance to spend just one night with Tony Ross, I would, and I bet you would have too! He's a dream. He looks like Antonio Banderas, only better!"

"Maybe I would have, but not now," said Lucy, staring at his picture.

Becky continued. "She must have met him somewhere. If it wasn't America or Italy, it must have been in London. After all she lived there."

"Yes, that's true."

"Look, your mum was young and single and pretty. She could have gone to a nightclub and met him there. He could have seduced her, then gone back to Italy to his wife and children. Your mum found she was pregnant, didn't want her friends to know, and sneaked off to Bishops Fell"

"That sounds more like it," replied Lucy. "I could believe that."

"I wonder why she picked this place?"

Lucy suddenly jumped up in her seat. "Of course!"

"What?"

"Years ago, Mum's sister Colette and Dad's sister Rachel were friends - they were both air-stewardesses together. If Aunt Colette mentioned to Aunt Rachel that Mum wanted to get away from London, Aunt Rachel could have found her a place here easily, because she came from here - and that's how she met Dad!"

"Of course, it's all so simple!"

Lucy was by now beginning to shake with excitement. She stared, fascinated, at the picture of Tony Ross, then looked across at her friend.

"Becky...do you really think that Tony Ross is my real father?"

"Yes, he must be. He's got the same name that's on your birth certificate, and he's a singer - and that's why your mum doesn't want you to go into showbusiness. I'll bet she's terrified that you'll bump into your father and your half-brothers."

"Of course!" gasped Lucy.

"You could have ended up having an affair or getting married to one of them."

"But that would be incest - that's disgusting!"

"Exactly!"

"God!" cried Lucy. "Why on earth didn't Mum tell me about this? How could she keep such a secret, and make me so miserable? I hate her!"

"Now, come on, Lucy, be fair. If your mum had told you, you would have gone over the top! You'd probably have gone rushing round telling everyone, have given your mum a load of grief and gone chasing round the world trying to find him."

Lucy suddenly started to giggle. She threw her head back and punched the roof of the car, the colour rushing to her face and her eyes sparkling.

"I'm the daughter of Tony Ross!" she shouted. "*I am the daughter of the most famous singer in the world...* Yahoo!"

When Lucy had finally calmed down, Becky became serious.

"Lucy, what are you going to do?"

Lucy looked again at the picture of Tony Ross, and with an index finger she gently stroked his face and hair.

"I'm going to meet him...if it takes me the rest of my life. I just want to speak to him...to be in his presence...even if it's only to say hello..."

"How?"

"I'm going to go professional - if I do well, I'm bound to meet up with him sooner or later."

"You're not going to tell him who you are?" asked Becky anxiously.

"No, It wouldn't be fair to his family. Don't worry, Bex, I won't let the cat out of the bag." Lucy paused. "I'm going to see Mrs Davis tonight, to see if she can get me an audition or put me in a talent show."

"In that case, we'd better get a move on, or we'll be late!" said Becky, starting up the car.

They drove on in silence. Lucy sat with her eyes closed, pressing the picture of Tony Ross against her pounding heart.

ELEVEN

LUCY GOES TO LONDON 1995/6

After rehearsals that night Lucy spoke to Joyce Davis about turning professional - she did not tell her about Tony Ross.

"Joyce, can you get me into a talent show?" Mrs Davis looked shocked. "Talent show? Oh no, Lucy."

"But why?"

"Because talent shows are for nightclubs, holiday camps and ships cruises. You're much too good for that. You'll need proper auditions and an agent."

"How do I do that?"

"Fortunately, Lucy, I come from a musical family, and I have a brother-in-law who is an agent in London. I'll have a word with him and get him to listen to you. With a bit of luck he might come up with a suitable part for you, and he'll let you know."

"Oh, thank you, thank you!" cried Lucy.

On the way home Lucy told Becky about her talk with Joyce Davis.

"Isn't it wonderful, Becky!"

"Lucy, I think it would be best if we both went to live in London. We could get a flat and jobs, and when your auditions come up you'll be on the spot."

"Oh, Bex, that would be brilliant!"

Lucy and Becky's parents were not happy about their daughters going to live in London, and Claudia looked ill. But at 22 years of age, the girls were quite old enough to do as they pleased, and their parents realised this.

Over the next few weeks, Bill helped the girls find accommodation there. It was very expensive, but through some contacts of Colette's, they found a flat to share with two air-stewardesses, who would not be around much. They had trips to London for the girls to have interviews with hairdressing salons, and by the end of the year it was agreed that Lucy and Becky would move to London after Christmas and New Year.

Life was hectic for the girls, trying to keep up with rehearsals for the Christmas show, packing belongings and arranging goodbye parties with friends and family. During the excitement Lucy was told that Joyce's brother-in-law, the agent Martin Davis, was coming to Cropwell for Christmas, and was prepared to hear Lucy sing. Her nerves were in shreds.

Martin went to watch the Christmas show at the Cropwell Theatre where Lucy was singing a variety of songs, such as "Music of the Night" from "Phantom of the Opera"; the heartbreaking song "Tell Me it's not True" from "Blood Brothers"; "I'm a Stranger in Paradise" from "Kismet" and "I Could Have Danced All Night" from "My Fair Lady".

After the show, he asked to see Lucy at Joyce's house where she sang for him again, while Joyce played the piano.

When she had finished, Lucy stared at him, her eyes wide, her fingers gripping her skirt. He looked up at her from his chair.

"I'm very impressed, Lucy."

"Can you get me into a show?" she asked anxiously.

"Here is my card, Lucy. Now I want you to send me your photograph. Keep up the singing and be patient. When a part comes up that I think will suit you I'll let you know, and I'll arrange for you to have an audition."

Lucy left Joyce's house on a cloud.

Christmas and New Year flew by, and it was soon time for Lucy and Becky to move to London. After some tearful goodbyes, they drove down in Becky's car, the boot and back seat laden with luggage. Bill had made Lucy promise that if she was ever short of money, she was to contact him immediately and he would put money into her bank account. She looked up at him, her eyes shimmering. She loved Bill; she loved his big, strong body and his kind, lined face and warm grey eyes, and soft grey hair, now thinning on top. She hugged him tightly.

"You're the best dad in the world," she whispered, feeling so full of guilt that she had broken her promise to him.

"Don't forget to ring us, Lucy. We'll miss you," begged Claudia.

Lucy looked at her mother's haggard face and drooping shoulders, and suddenly felt so sorry for her that she gave her a big hug.

"Don't worry, Mum, I will, and we'll be O.K. We won't do anything stupid, like taking drugs or anything..." She nearly said, "I won't get pregnant" but managed to stop herself.

Lucy got into Becky's car, and waved to her unhappy parents.

They set off for London. They were so excited, they sang all the way, mainly to tapes of Tony Ross. Lucy had hardly stopped playing his songs for weeks, she so much wanted to hear her father's voice. As it was a Sunday the roads were not too busy, and they made good time.

They arrived in London at lunchtime, at a tall house with a flight of steps leading up to the front door, and railings on each side. The house had been turned into flats, and they were to share the top one. It consisted of a small kitchen, a bathroom, lounge and four bedrooms. The rooms were fully furnished - all they needed was their own bed linen and towels. The girls spent the afternoon unpacking in the quiet flat, as their room-mates were both away. In the evening they both went out for a meal and a drink.

Lucy and Becky started their new jobs on the Monday morning. They had been lucky enough to get jobs in the same large salon.

They adored London and soon made friends, though they hardly saw the two air-stewardesses, who were both tall, glamorous and tended to mix with their own friends.

The weeks flew by, and it was in May that Lucy got her first phone call from Martin Davis.

She squealed in excitement.

"What's happened?"

"Oh, Becky, I've got my first audition!"

"Tell me!"

"Well, you've heard of Sir John Phillips?"

"Of course!"

"Well, he's written a musical based on the story "Gone With the Wind". He's called it 'Scarlet' and I've got an audition for it!"

"Oh, Lucy, how wonderful!"

"It's opening in September!"

"When's your audition?"

"A week on Monday, at 2 p.m. Martin Davis is going to send me the details through the post. Gosh, I must ring Joyce.!"

As the audition drew close, Lucy was in a state of delirium. She had been given a list of songs and had to choose two. She'd also been told to wear something smart and formal, as John Phillips did not like people turning up to his auditions looking scruffy, or wearing jeans and trainers.

Joyce Davis came down for the weekend before the audition to coach Lucy. Becky had also taken the day off to watch the audition and do Lucy's make-up and hair.

Lucy had bought a plain but slinky red dress with matching shoes. Her eyes looked enormous and her hair was like black silk shining on top of her head, two long tendrils falling in front of her ears.

"Oh, Lucy," gasped Becky, "you look just like Audrey Hepburn!"

"True," laughed Joyce, "but our Lucy has got a better voice!"

Laughing, the three of them made their way downstairs to get a taxi to take them to the theatre.

When they walked into the theatre, Lucy felt sick with nerves. She looked round, soaking up the atmosphere which she loved. There were a lot of people sitting round waiting. It was the second week of the auditions. Towards the middle of the auditorium some seats had been removed and in their place was a long table where three people were seated. In the middle sat Sir John Phillips, looking handsome with a head of golden curls and watchful grey eyes. His face was serious with a straight nose and a neat mouth and teeth. Although he was only 32, his success with music had been phenomenal.

Lucy sat nervously with Joyce and Becky, watching the other singers performing. Some of them only sang one song, before being asked to leave the stage. She didn't notice Martin Davis walk down the aisle and settle himself behind her.

Lucy's stomach was churning, and when her name was called she jumped. She got up and walked towards the stage, where she was approached by a lady who checked her name against a list and asked what two songs she would be singing. The lady spoke to the orchestra as Lucy gracefully climbed up the steps and onto the stage.

John Phillips watched her as she walked onto the stage. She was the most beautiful girl he had ever seen - she took his breath away.

As soon as the first notes of the song began to play, her heart began to lift and she sang so beautifully that the whole theatre fell silent as her voice floated gloriously over their heads.

By the time Lucy had finished, John Phillips had fallen hopelessly in love with her. His serious face hid the emotion that was churning inside him.

Lucy crept back to her seat.

"You were marvellous, Lucy," whispered Becky.

"Well done, my dear," said Joyce, smiling and patting Lucy's knee.

Lucy felt a tap on her shoulder and saw Martin's face smiling at her.

"If you don't get a part in this production - I'll emigrate!" he grinned.

When the auditions were over, a lady thanked them all for coming and said they would be contacted shortly. Then, to Lucy's surprise, the lady, wearing a dark suit and a white blouse, came up to her.

"Lucilla Lane? Would you mind waiting behind for a few minutes? Sir John would like to speak to you."

"Of course," stammered Lucy. She looked at Joyce and Becky. "What does he want?" she asked.

"To offer you a part, I expect," laughed Joyce happily.

When the other applicants had gone, Sir John Phillips approached Lucy. He was slightly taller than her and his grey eyes smiled down at her as he shook her hand.

"Miss Lane?"

"Yes."

"Is this your first audition?"

"Yes, it is."

"I thought I hadn't seen you before." Lucy was trembling. "Miss Lane, I would like to offer you the part of Scarlette O'Hara."

"Scarlette O'Hara! How wonderful!"

"Then you accept?" he smiled.

"Oh, yes, yes please!"

"Good. Now, we start rehearsals in August and open in September. My secretary will contact you with all the details including getting you measured for your costumes."

"Oh, thank you!" beamed Lucy.

"Until August - when we meet again. Goodbye."

"Goodbye," murmured Lucy.

And Sir John Phillips was gone.

Lucy was stunned. "He's offered me the leading role."

"Well done, Lucy!"

"Congratulations, my dear!"

"Well done, young lady!"

Lucy left the theatre in a daze. Joyce, Becky and Martin took her home to change, and they all went out to celebrate.

The weeks that followed were hectic. Joyce sent Lucy a video of "Gone with the Wind" so that she could learn the story and get to learn the character of the vivacious, wicked Scarlette O'Hara. She was still busy working at the salon and her boss was good enough to let take time off to go and sign her contract and have her costume fittings.

Lucy was thrilled with all her lovely hats and crinoline dresses. There was a white one covered in frills, a green and white one, a wedding dress and a black dress for when Scarlette's husband dies, plus many more beautiful gowns, all cleverly made for quick changes.

Carpenters and electricians were working on the sets for the spectacular show. There was the lounge in the beautiful house at Tara; special effects made the stage look as if it was on fire during the war scenes; and there was the grand staircase, where at the very end Scarlette would collapse, weeping when Rhett Butler walked out on her with those famous words,"Frankly, my dear, I don't give a damn."

In August, as rehearsals were due to begin, Lucy began to panic.

"Becky - these rehearsals - we only get three weeks! I'll never be ready!"

"You'll be O.K. Lucy, don't worry. You're a professional now. In Cropwell we did two shows and a Christmas show, and we had weeks of rehearsals - but only two nights a week. You'll be rehearsing all day!"

On Lucy's last day at the salon all the staff went out for the evening and Lucy was showered with gifts and 'good luck' cards, and given a bouquet of flowers. The staff all drank a toast to her.

"To Lucy!" they cried out. "We wish you all the best and hope you become a star!" Lucy was deeply touched.

Lucy arrived at her first rehearsal with trembling legs. When she arrived, the theatre seemed full of people. There was a large cast, many of them playing two roles. There was a buzz of excitement as the cast started chatting to each other. Lucy felt lonely until a fat, jolly, black American lady approached her.

"Hi, honey, you must be Lucilla Lane."

"Yes, I am," replied Lucy shyly.

"Well, I'm Winifred Jones, known as Skinny Winnie, and I play your big, fat Nanny!" Lucy laughed.

"Come and meet the others." She took Lucy over to meet some of the main characters. There was Nick Morrison, who was playing the handsome Rhett Butler - tall, dark and handsome, with a freshly-grown moustache making him look just like the famous Clark Gable. She was then introduced to Andrea Bond, who was playing the part of the sweet, gentle Melanie and was also to be Lucy's understudy. Andrea was the same height as Lucy, a thin girl with large brown eyes, short, black, spiky hair and an earring in her small nose - she reminded Lucy of a pet monkey. Julia White and Kay Archer were playing the parts of Scarlette's sisters; they were both slim girls with brown hair, Julia's smooth and straight and Kay's curly.

Lucy then went on to meet Christopher Fellows, who was tall and fair-haired and studious-looking - just like his character, Ashley Wilkes.

"Hello, Lucy, nice to meet. Now don't forget you have to be madly in love with me all through this show."

"I'll try," giggled Lucy.

"Hello there, young lady. You won't be madly in love with me, I play your father."

"Nice to meet you, Mr. O'Hara," she replied sweetly. Mr. O'Hara was being played by Daniel Day, a well-known singer - short and stocky with light brown wavy hair, a droopy moustache and twinkling blue eyes.

The buzz of conversation suddenly stopped. Lucy turned round to see Sir John Phillips leading a group of people, including the producer, towards them. He then introduced everybody, chatted about the musical and how he wanted it presented. When he had finished, he introduced Lucy, much to her embarrassment.

"I'd like you all to meet Lucilla Lane. This is Lucy's first professional performance, but as she has sung for many years as an amateur, she does know the ropes and the procedures, but not you, so please, all of you, make her welcome." He smiled across at Lucy and she blushed.

"Thank you." The buzz of conversation started up again.

"You O.K. Lucy?" asked Andrea.

"Yes, thanks, isn't he gorgeous?"

"John Phillips?"

"Yes."

"Well don't waste your time on him. His first love is music, women always come second," she whispered.

"He's not gay is he?"

"No, but Christopher Fellows is!" The two of them giggled.

The rehearsals began.

Lucy adapted to her role like a duck to water. All the experience she had gained at the Cropwell Theatre stood her in good stead. She loved the songs which poured out of her effortlessly. She was a true natural on the stage and got on well with everyone. She made special friends with Andrea, and they worked well together on stage.

The whole cast loved the musical, and put their hearts and souls into it. They became like a family all working together.

As the opening night drew near Lucy could hardly sleep for excitement. Her biggest worry was the press reviews.

"Becky, it's going to be in the papers - what if Mum and Dad see it? They'll be fuming."

"Perhaps you'd better warn them," suggested Becky.

"Yes, I'd better. Mum will hate me."

"Lucy, your mum does not, and never will hate you. I don't know where you get that silly idea from. We know the reason she doesn't want you to sing. She might be angry but she does not hate you."

"Yes, Bex, you're right. I'll phone."

Lucy rang home.

"Hi, Mark."

"Hi, Lucy how you doing?"

"I'm fine thanks, little brother! Is Dad there?"

"He sure is. I'll get him."

Bill was on the line. "Hello, sweetheart, how are you?"

"I'm fine, Dad, everything's wonderful."

"That's great."

"Er...Dad...I've got a confession to make."

"What's that, love?"

"I've broken my promise to you."

"I see...well, cough it up."

"I've got a part in a London show - I've got the leading role."

"I see..."

"Dad, don't be angry - the show opens on Monday and I'm already as nervous as Hell."

"I'm not angry, Lucy. With a voice like yours it was bound to happen sooner or later."

"But, Dad, you've never heard me sing!"

"I have, Lucy, many times."

"But when, where?"

"The Cropwell Theatre, of course."

"You've been to see me?" she squeaked.

"A number of times, but don't tell your mother!"

"Oh, Dad, you are wicked!" cried Lucy.

"I went to see you in 'West Side Story' - after that I was hooked, and I've been to every show since. You don't need to tell me how good you are, love, I know."

"What about Mum. She'll kill me. Are you going to tell her?"

"I don't know yet. I'll have to think about it."

They talked a little longer, and Lucy told him all about "Scarlette" before ringing off.

She turned to Becky. "My dad is the best dad in the world!"

The show was ready at last and the first performance was ready to start. The cast were all nervous and Lucy had taken some extra honey to soothe her throat. The first ones to appear were waiting in the wings. They were almost unrecognisable in their costumes - particularly Andrea whose spiky hair was now covered in a wig of long, brown hair swept into a bun and ringlets, the earring gone from her nose.

The orchestra were plucking at their strings and tuning up and the auditorium was buzzing with chatter as critics and journalists mixed in with a music-loving audience.

John Phillips, looking devastatingly handsome in his evening suit, appeared from the orchestra pit and the overture began. The rich, red curtain gently rose into the flies above. "Scarlette" had begun.

The musical was a resounding success. The audience were captivated by the whole spectacular show, and they adored Lucy. Everyone watched fascinated as the story unfolded, right up until the end, when Scarlette O'Hara collapsed weeping on the grand staircase, and the rest of the cast, hiding in the wings, began to sing a heart-stirring song, "Tomorrow is another day", their voices rising into a blood-tingling crescendo.

The audience went wild, standing up and cheering in the aisles and shouting for more curtain calls. Becky and Joyce were in floods of tears.

Sir John Philips took a smiling bow on behalf of the orchestra and Lucy was given an enormous bouquet of flowers, her face glowing, her eyes sparkling like diamonds.

She was a star.

TWELVE

A SHOCK FOR LUCY 1997

Claudia sat on the settee with Bill, her head bowed, her hands fiddling with her Gemini necklace.

"I'm sorry, Claudia."

"It was bound to happen sooner or later," she replied sadly. "She's like Attilio. He used to say that singing was in his blood and he couldn't live without his music. He could live without me, but not that."

"What shall we do?"

"I don't know, Bill. Just the thought of her ever meeting him makes me feel ill."

"I think we should tell her before it's too late."

"I'm too scared."

"I suggest we keep tracks on Tony Ross, and if we hear that he's coming to London - then she'll have to be told."

Claudia agreed.

Meanwhile, down in London, Lucy was having a wonderful life. She was doing what she wanted most to do - sing, sing and sing. The cast were like a family to her and she adored them all. Her favourites were Andrea ('pet monkey') and "Skinny Winnie", who reminded her of Whoopie Goldberg with her lively personality and her big, toothy smile. Winnie had a rich contralto voice which harmonised perfectly with Lucy and Andrea's soprano voices.

By the following March, "Scarlette" had been running successfully to packed houses every night, and Lucy felt she was living in a wonderful dream. But one day that dream came face to face with a shocking reality.

It was a Friday evening and word was flying round the dressing rooms that John Phillips wanted a meeting with the cast after the show.

"What do you think it's about?" Lucy asked Andrea.

"Probably a change of cast," replied Andrea airily.

After the final curtain call the cast waited on stage for John Phillips.

He came on to the stage, smiling, his hands raised.

"Right, everyone, I have some exciting news for you all. First of all, I'm sorry to say that we are going to lose our Rhett Butler – Nick is going to take the lead in a new opera. We all wish him the best of luck in his new role."

The cast cheered and some of them patted Nick on the back.

"The good news is that the Denver Brothers are coming to take his place. They are contracted for one year."

There were cheers from the cast, but Lucy was thunderstruck.

"As you know the twins, Clay and Leo, are inseparable and share all performances. Audiences love them as they are all trying to guess which twin they have watched, and have to wait for the curtain call to find out. The pair of them are a bit wild, and will sometimes both appear in the same performance, confusing everyone - so watch out, Lucy!"

Lucy's cheeks were crimson, and she nervously swept a hand over her shoulder as if to push her hair back.

John Phillips continued. "The twins will be arriving in two weeks time. Then there will be three weeks of rehearsals for them to learn their parts. They're very quick to learn and are certain that they'll be ready when Nick leaves; if not Nick's understudy can take over."

The cast were buzzing with excitement at the news, but when John Phillips looked across at Lucy's rapturous face, his heart sank.

"Now, girls," he continued, "the Denvers have quite a reputation, so be careful!" There followed hoots of laughter and some ribald comments.

Lucy couldn't get back to her flat fast enough to tell Becky. She ran up the stairs and crashed through the door, shouting, "Becky, Becky, where are you? Becky!" She ran into the living room where Becky was sitting curled up on the settee with a coffee after having an evening out with the girls from the salon.

"Lucy, what's happened?"

"Oh, Becky, you'll never guess - the Denver Brothers are coming to the show!"

"What! Oh, Lucy!"

"They'll be here in two weeks. Oh, Becky - I'm so excited! I'm going to meet my half-brothers already and I thought I'd have to wait years and years!"

"Lucy, you'll have to be careful!"

"Don't worry, I won't tell them who I am. Oh, I'm so happy and so scared - I wonder what they'll be like?"

The two girls sat chatting non-stop about Lucy's exciting news.

As the day drew near for the twins' arrival, Lucy started to panic. It had finally sunk in that these two famous men were the sons of the great Tony Ross, and her half-brothers. What would they say if they knew that their father had had an affair with her mother, and that she was their half-sister? Her stomach started to churn at the thought that soon she would be singing with them and then having to kiss them on stage. Whatever would her mother say?"

Lucy and Becky had been back to Cropwell for a couple of visits during the last few months, where friends, family and Maureen and Rose made such a fuss of them. She had noticed her mother was looking paler and thinner.

"She must be so worried about me ever meeting Tony Ross or his sons," thought Lucy. "On my next visit I think I'd better tell her I know, and then she can stop worrying."

Monday morning arrived and Lucy was more nervous than she had ever been in her life at the prospect of meeting Clay and Leo Denver. Her heart missed a beat when she saw them for the first time, sauntering down the aisle together in black jeans and white polo-neck sweaters which looked fabulous against their sun tans, black hair and deep brown eyes. Some of the girls in the cast were almost swooning, but Lucy just stared at them in frozen fascination.

"Hi, everyone!" they smiled, their perfect teeth white, their eyes sparkling with mischief.

John Phillips introduced them to the cast and when they came up to Lucy to shake her hand and speak to her, she thought she was going to faint. They were so handsome!

John Phillips was not too happy when he saw the effect the Denvers had on Lucy. His heart contracted in pain and he frowned. Before rehearsal began, he spoke to them both.

"Lads, Lucy is new to all this and she is my star - so don't piss her about!"

"O.K. John, don't get your knickers in a twist - we'll behave!" they both laughed.

How Lucy got through her rehearsals with the Denvers, she didn't know. It was only her skill as an actress that stopped them knowing how nervous she was.

Everyone loved working with Clay and Leo, and Winnie adored them. "Lucy, dem boys sure are bootiful!"

Lucy soon discoverd the difference between the boys. Clay was a little more reserved, cautious and polite than Leo who was outgoing, bossy and utterly outrageous.

After two weeks of rehearsals Lucy had grown used to them and her churning heart had finally settled down to a steady beat. But not for long...

On that Saturday night, after the show most of the cast decided to go on to a nightclub to celebrate with the Denvers. At about 2 a.m, Lucy found herself standing next to Clay, and they got chatting, their heads close together so that they could hear each other above the noise.

Lucy was curious about Tony Ross's wife.

"Is your mother still alive, Clay?"

"No, she died when we were very young."

"Oh, I'm sorry. Do you remember her?"

"No, but we have a picture of her at home. She was English, like you, and she had long blonde hair and blue eyes. She was very beautiful. I'm named after her," he added proudly.

"With a name like Clay?" she laughed.

"No, no, my name is really Claudio - her name was Claudia, and she was a twin like me and Leo."

Lucy couldn't believe her ears. She thought she must have heard wrong.

"What did you say?" she shouted in his ear.

"Claudia C.L.A.U.D.I.A."

Lucy froze. She was shaken to the core. Before Clay had time to notice the shock he had just given her, he was dragged onto the dance floor by Andrea.

Lucy turned with trembling legs and made her way to the 'Ladies.' She dashed into a cubicle, put down the toilet lid, and sat on the toilet, putting her elbows on her trembling knees. She buried her head in her hands. She was in such a state of shock, she could hardly think straight.

Her mother had not had an affair with Tony Ross...she had been his wife! She was the mother of the Denver twins! She must have run away... But why? How could she have left two little boys? It was too awful to be true. Lucy's head was reeling.

She had sat there for a long time, her head in her hands, when she heard Winnie calling.

"Lucy, honey, you in there?"

Lucy slowly came out of the cubicle to find an anxious Winnie staring at her.

"What's wrong, honey, you look real pale?"

"I… I've got a terrible headache," mumbled Lucy.

"Come with me, baby," Winnie cooed, collecting Lucy's bag and jacket. Soon she was putting her in a taxi.

When Lucy got home, the flat was in darkness. She banged on Becky's door, praying she wasn't still out.

"Becky... Becky!" she cried.

"What's up?" shouted Becky, sitting up and putting on her

bedside lamp. Lucy charged through the door, sat on Becky's bed and burst into tears. Becky put an arm round her friend's shaking shoulders.

"Lucy, whatever's wrong?"

"My... my... mum..." sobbed Lucy.

"What's happened?"

"She... she... was... T..Tony Ross's... wife!"

"She was *what*?"

"T...Tony Ross's... w..wife!"

"Lucy, you've got to be kidding!"

"No... no... it's true!"

"Lucy…how did you find out?"

Between sobs and sniffs Lucy told Becky about her conversation with Clay Denver.

"I can't believe it!" gasped Becky.

"Nor me... Oh, Bex, how could she have been married to that wonderful man and had two beautiful sons, and then walk out on them? How could she have been so cruel?"

"She must have had a good reason, Lucy."

"Oh, sure. She must have run off with my dad!" snapped Lucy, tossing her head and pushing her hair back over her shoulders.

"Lucy, we must try and think logically. First - the reason she left. Now, Tony Ross has had more women than we've had hot dinners, so he may have been unfaithful to her, and she wouldn't have stood for that."

"That figures, but then how did she meet Dad, when he was in Cropwell and she was in Italy?"

"Well, she either knew him before she met Tony Ross and went to him for help, or she could have met him in Italy when he was, perhaps, on holiday there."

"That's possible, but why leave the boys?"

"Lucy, she couldn't just walk out of Italy with them, they may not have even had passports. It would have taken a full-scale operation to get two little boys out of the country, and she must have been expecting you. You were born in England, but your mum put Tony's name on your birth certificate, so there's no doubt you're his child." Lucy nodded.

"Perhaps," suggested Becky, "your mum and Bill went off together and prepared a home for the twins - they would have needed cots, pushchairs, highchairs, clothes and all sorts of things, and then applied for custody. But Tony Ross may have said 'sod off' and taken them to America."

"Of course!" cried Lucy. "And she wouldn't know where they were!"

"That's right - and these custody battles can go on for years - and in the meantime she has you and later she has Mark and Luke. By this time Clay and Leo wouldn't even remember her or know who she was, so she gave up."

"Becky, I think you must be right - you're so clever!"

"That's why your mum and dad have never got married, Lucy. Legally she's probably still Tony Ross's wife."

"Oh, Becky, this is all so unbelievable, and why my mum never told me I'll never know. I'll never forgive her, never!"

"Oh, Lucy don't cry!"

"I feel sick, and I've got a terrible headache," groaned Lucy.

"Look, you get yourself to bed and I'll bring you a warm drink and some painkillers."

"Thanks, Bex. You're a real pal."

Later that night, Becky lay in the darkness listening to the March wind howling outside, and the odd car drive past far below her. She, too, was too shocked to sleep.

The two girls had a lie-in on the Sunday morning, and spent the day talking about Claudia being married to Tony Ross, and of all the possible reasons why she had run away.

There was now one week left of rehearsals with the Denver Brothers before they took over the role of Rhett Butler.

Lucy felt more nervous and anxious than she ever had before in her whole life. Every time she looked at Clay and Leo, she thought, "Their mother is my mother," and her insides would turn somersaults. She wondered how she was ever going to get through the next 12 months, performing with them on stage, afraid to tell them who she was.

On the Thursday during rehearsals, something happened which made Lucy want to turn and simply run away.

She and Leo were standing in the wings, towards the end of the performance, when he put an arm round her shoulders and spoke softly in her ear.

"Lucy, honey, you are so beautiful."

"Oh, thank you, Leo," she replied shakily.

"Lucy, why don't you have dinner with me tonight after the show?" He began to slide a hand gently over her bottom. "Then we could spend the night together - you won't regret it." He began kissing her neck.

Lucy was horrified, and pushed him away. "Sorry, I'm spoken for," she replied tartly and then hearing her cue, she tossed her head and swept onto the stage.

Lucy was in turmoil. She knew she couldn't go on performing with the Denvers. As soon as the rehearsal was over, she went up to John Phillips.

"John, can I have a word in private?"

"Of course, we'll go to my office, come along." The two of them walked in silence to his office. He closed the door and turned to face her.

"Now, Lucy, what's the matter?" he asked kindly.

"I can't go on!" she cried.

"But why?"

"I've got to leave here. I've got to get away!"

John looked in puzzlement at the frightened eyes in her distraught face, and her trembling hands.

"Lucy, you're my star, I can't just let you go!" He put his slender hands on her shoulders and looked into her eyes. "Now tell me exactly what's wrong."

"It's... it's... Leo!" she cried. "He made a pass at me!"

John Phillips tried hard not to smile.

"Oh, Lucy, you're a very beautiful girl, these things are bound to happen."

Lucy started to cry, and the tears began to slide down her pale face. "But it's not right!"

"Not right?"

"No...he's...my brother!"

"Your brother! Lucy, what on earth are you talking about?" John asked, baffled.

"It's...t...true - but he doesn't know."

"Lucy, I think you'd better explain," he said quietly.

Between sniffs and sobs, Lucy told John how she'd made her discovery. John Phillips looked at her in amazement. He could hardly believe what he was hearing, but was more than thankful that the Denvers were Lucy's brothers and not her lovers. He looked down at her with warm, gentle eyes.

"Good God, my dear Lucy, now are you quite sure about all this?"

"Yes, I've got my birth certificate with Tony Ross's real name and Clay said that their mother was called Claudia. It's too much of a coincidence."

John ran a hand over his mouth and chin and frowned. "Mmmmm…Tony's real name is Attilio Rossini - I know that for a fact, and I believe he did some of his training here...which means that they could have married here..."

"I could search for their marriage certificate!" gasped Lucy.

"I'll come with you, we'll go now, come on!" John snatched up a black raincoat and a pair of dark glasses. "Lucy, let your hair down, we don't want to be recognised." Lucy untied her dark hair and let it fall round her face.

John took her hand and they hurried to the back of the stage, where Lucy grabbed her coat and bag from the dressing room. On the way out, they bumped into the Denver brothers. John glared at Leo.

"I warned you about Lucy - now it's hands off, is that clear?" Clay and Leo looked uncomfortable. They had never seen John Phillips look so angry. Leo looked at Lucy.

"I'm sorry, Lucy, I didn't mean to offend you."

She blushed, but before she could answer him, John Phillips snapped at Leo.

"You touch her again, and you're finished! Come along, Darling." He tugged Lucy's hand and they hurried out of the stage door and looked for a taxi, as John's chauffeur was not there. John grinned and looked at Lucy.

"That's sorted them out - they won't bother you if they think you're my girlfriend!"

"Oh, thank you!" cried Lucy. "But how do you tell them apart when they're just standing there?"

"Leo has always got that arrogant look in his eyes - here's a taxi, come on!"

Within a few minutes the taxi had dropped them at St. Catherine's House, and they made their way through the glass doors to the marriage section. On their way, Lucy spotted notices saying that St. Catherine's House would soon be closing and re-opening at a new place in July, called the Family Record Centre.

John looked at Lucy.

"I'm trying to work out how old Clay and Leo are," he said. "I think they're about 27 - so they would have been born about 1970. Shall we start there and work back?"

"O.K."

It took no more than a few minutes for them to find the entry of the marriage of Claudia Morris to Attilio Rossini, in the September quarter of 1970.

"It's true," whispered Lucy, tears welling up in her big brown eyes. "It's really true!"

John put an arm round her shoulders. "Shall we order it?"

"Yes...yes." Lucy filled out the form for her mother's marriage certificate and was told she could collect it on the Saturday morning. She looked up at John as they left the building.

"My friend Becky and I came here to find my birth certificate. While we were here, we looked for my mum's marriage certificate to my dad, but we couldn't find it. If I'd gone back a few more years I would have found her marriage to Attilio Rossini."

John smiled. "Never mind, Lucy. Better late than never!"

"Yes, that's true."

He took her hand. "You've had quite a few shocks over the last couple of years."

"Yes, I have - it's all knocked me for six!"

"Don't worry, Lucy. I'll look after you."

"I don't want to be a nuisance to you," she lied.

"You'll never be that, Lucy." And her insides turned over.

John looked at his watch. "We've just got time for a bite to eat and a drink before we have to get back for tonight's performance."

Holding hands, they walked towards Covent Garden, chatting earnestly together.

On the Saturday morning, John picked up Lucy from her flat. She showed him her birth certificate while his chauffeur drove them to Kingsway. John studied it.

"Tony has kept very quiet about his wife all these years. Everyone thinks she died," he murmured.

"Tomorrow morning I'm going to visit my mother and have it out with her - and she'd better tell me the truth!"

Lucy was trembling with nerves as she queued up for the certificate. "I'm almost too scared to open it," she whispered in a choked voice.

With shaking fingers, she opened it out, and with John's blond curls pressed against her dark, silky hair, they read it together. Lucy read some of it out in a choked voice.

"... 20th July, 1970... Attilio Giovanni Rossini...bachelor...full age... a singer... father... Flavio Rossini... business man (deceased)... Claudia Morris..spinster... full age... secretary... father...Mark Morris... tour guide...(deceased)... witness... Colette Morris..."

Lucy stifled a sob and put a hand over her mouth.

"Is it your mother's?" asked John quietly.

"Yes... it is my mum... My aunt, Colette was a witness. Oh, God - I still can't believe it!"

With an arm round her shoulders, John Phillips took Lucy home to her flat.

Tomorrow she would learn the whole truth.

THIRTEEN

CONFESSION 1997

On the Sunday morning, Lucy and Becky got up early, had a quick breakfast and packed an overnight bag for their visit to Cropwell. Lucy was in a panic. Her clothes, as usual, were flung everywhere and she grumbled and moaned as she hunted for clean underwear, jeans and tops.

When they were both ready, they made their way downstairs and got into Becky's car, throwing their bags on the back seat. The precious birth and marriage certificate were tucked into Lucy's bag.

"Becky, I'm scared. Whatever will my mum say?"

"She'll have no choice but to tell you the truth, and don't forget, if things go badly, ring me and I'll come and fetch you."

"O.K. and if things are alright, I'll let you know and we'll come back tomorrow morning."

Lucy found herself shaking all the way home, and when they drew close to Cropwell, she started to feel sick.

When they pulled up outside Chimneys, she got out of the car, her legs trembling.

"Good luck, Lucy."

"Thanks, Bex."

Carrying her overnight bag, Lucy walked up to the house and let herself in, dropping her bags on the living room floor. She found her parents in the kitchen. They looked up at her in surprise.

"Lucy! How lovely to see you!"

Lucy stared at her mother, her dark eyes flashing.

"Why didn't you tell me that you were married to Tony Ross, and that I am his daughter?"

Claudia gasped with shock and started to buckle at the knees.

Bill picked her up in his arms and glared at Lucy, angrily. "Lucy, you don't know what you've done!"

He carried Claudia into the living room and sat her on the settee. Lucy followed, frowning - what was the matter with her parents? What was all the fuss? Why did they look so alarmed?

"Get your mother a brandy!" shouted Bill, and as an afterthought added, "and get yourself one, you're going to need it!"

Lucy's heart skipped a beat. Whatever was wrong? How awful was the truth going to be?

With trembling hands, she poured two brandies, walked over to the settee and stood staring at her parents.

"It's alright, darling." Bill's face was full of concern, and Claudia's looked grey and ill. Lucy realised that she had given her mother a terrible shock.

Bill took a brandy from Lucy and gave it to Claudia, who sipped it slowly, the colour coming back into her cheeks.

"You'll have to tell her, darling."

"Yes, I know."

Bill looked at Lucy. "You'd better sit down, Lucy. Your mother has something to tell you."

Lucy sat down beside her mother and Bill went into the kitchen to prepare the Sunday lunch and to wait for Mark and Luke to come in after their football training.

Lucy stared as her mother's ashen face, not knowing what to say. Claudia put a hand over Lucy's and looked at her with sad, frightened blue eyes.

"Lucy, this is very difficult for me, but I'm going to tell you everything - but you must promise me that if you ever meet Tony Ross, you won't tell him who you are."

"I promise," replied Lucy softly, still utterly mystified.

Claudia told Lucy everything, starting from the time when she first met Attilio, the death of her parents and her marriage and life in Italy. She told her about the cruelty of her in-laws when Attilio was away and her love for her little boys she hardly ever saw. She went on to tell Lucy about the day that her mother-in-law had hit her, and of Bruno putting a knife to her throat, and his menacing whisper of "Mafia."

Lucy listened in horror, tears welling up in her eyes. By the time Claudia had told her about her escape to England and the ensuing months, Lucy was breaking her heart.

"Oh, Mum," she cried, "why didn't you tell me?"

"Oh, Lucy," sobbed Claudia," I just couldn't! I didn't want you to know what a coward I was. I couldn't tell you about Claudy and Tilly. I know how you love children and I thought you would never forgive me."

"Oh, Mum, you must have been so frightened!" cried Lucy.

"I was. I still am, Lucy. If his family had ever found me they would probably cut my throat and take you away from me - the thought has terrified me since the day you were born."

"Oh, Mum," sobbed Lucy, "I've been so horrid to you all these years! I'm so sorry, can you ever forgive me?"

"Of course, darling. I love you and I'd forgive you anything."

"Mum, I don't know what to say."

Mother and daughter wept in each other's arms.

Eventually Lucy sat up and wiped away the tears with her hands.

"Mum, I love the dad I've got. If I had ever known Tony Ross, there would be no way I'd have gone to Italy and left you both behind."

"Oh, Lucy," Claudia smiled through her tears. "You've never met him. He could charm the birds out of the trees - he could seduce women just with his eyes. You wouldn't have stood a chance."

Lucy looked at her mother with new eyes. "Thanks for telling me, Mum, and I won't let you down."

The two women sipped their brandies and Claudia lit a cigarette, then looked at Lucy.

"How did you find out?"

"You won't like it, Mum."

"Never mind, just tell me the truth."

Lucy did.

Now it was Claudia's turn to look amazed as Lucy began her story.

"You've known all this time?"

"Yes, but I thought you'd had an affair with Tony Ross until..."

"Until what?" Lucy told her mother about the Denver Brothers.

"You've met Claudy and Tilly?"

"Yes."

"Oh, my God!" cried Claudia. "How are they? Are they alright? What are they like?"

"They are very handsome and very talented."

"And Tilly made a pass at you? The naughty boy!"

Lucy giggled. "Honestly, Mum, I nearly died. I went to John Phillips to give in my notice, but he got the truth out of me."

"Goodness, Lucy, how many people have you told?" cried Claudia.

"It's alright, Mum, only Becky and John Phillips know, and they won't say anything."

Claudia looked at Lucy earnestly. "Lucy - my boys, they're alright aren't they? It broke my heart to leave them behind. I've never got over it." She started to weep again, and Lucy hugged her.

"Mum, please don't cry, I can't bear it!" wept Lucy.

"I'm sorry, Lucy. but my life has been one long nightmare since I left Italy, and every time I see Attilio on the T.V. or in the papers, it brings it all back – there's been no escape. I don't know what I would have done without Bill, he saved my sanity."

Lucy pulled her mother's head down onto her shoulder and stroked her short blonde hair.

"It's going to be alright, Mum, don't cry." They clung to each other again. Lucy had never seen her mother so distressed, and it was breaking her heart to see it. The story her mother had told her had shocked her to the core.

Eventually Lucy sat up straight - her face lighting up.

"Mum, I've got a brilliant idea!"

"What's that, darling?"

"Why don't you come and see us?"

"See you?"

"Yes. Me and Claudy and Tilly. You could come and see us all singing together!"

"Oh, Lucy...I...I..couldn't."

"Of course you could. You could come and see the show and go home afterwards. No-one will know who you are. Tilly and Claudy think you're dead. Even if they saw you, they wouldn't know. Please, Mum!"

"Lucy, I'd love to, but I'm scared."

"Wait here," ordered Lucy as she dashed to her bag. Rummaging through, she fished out a programme and gave it to Claudia.

"This is a new programme. They're all ready for Monday when the Denver Brothers take over."

Claudia wiped her eyes and with trembling fingers took the programme off Lucy. On the front was a picture of Lucy in a white crinoline dress, her dark hair swept up in a swathe of ringlets, and the faces of Claudy and Tilly, with their hair swept back and wearing black moustaches, pictured in a circle. Claudia's eyes opened wide as she looked through the programme and saw full length pictures of her two sons, and an article about their careers.

"Oh, Lucy," she whispered, "don't they look handsome!"

"They are, Mum, and you can see them in the flesh. I can get you complimentary tickets. The best night would be a Saturday. It's the one night of the week I can guarantee that they'll role-share. You can see them both."

"Yes...yes...I'll come."

The two women hugged each other and began chatting excitedly.

"Mum," Lucy suddenly asked shyly, "have you still got those photos and things you brought out of Italy?"

"Of course."

"Can I see them?"

Claudia suddenly smiled and took Lucy's hand. "Come on, they're upstairs."

Hand in hand, Claudia and Lucy crept upstairs, making their way through the dining room and up the winding staircase to Claudia's bedroom. Lucy sat on the edge of the big double bed, while her mother went to a small safe in the wall and brought out a big chocolate box with a pink satin bow across the lid. She sat down beside Lucy and carefully removed the lid.

"I keep them all in here," she whispered. Lucy's heart was hammering against her ribs.

The first item Claudia took out was the wedding photo of herself and Attilio.

"Oh, Mum," gasped Lucy, "what a beautiful picture!" she gazed at it in amazement, unable to take her eyes from the sight of her lovely young mother smiling up at a young and handsome Tony Ross.

"I still can't believe you were married to Tony Ross, Mum, and he's my father! It's like a dream." She looked across at Claudia.

"Do you still love him, Mum?"

"Not really, Lucy. It's been a long time, and love does fade away. But I don't hate him, either. It all seems like a dream to me now."

"Do you regret leaving him?"

"No, Lucy. At the time it was now or never. If I had stayed, things would have got harder. He would have been away most of the time and I would have been left with his awful family and had a lot more children. It was hard enough leaving two, I couldn't have walked out leaving half a dozen!"

"That Bruno sounds a real brute. I'd like to kill him!" stormed Lucy. "And that Isabella wasn't much better!"

Claudia suddenly laughed.

"What's so funny?"

"Isabella the 'Sulk'"

"What about her?"

"Oh, Lucy, every time you have a sulk, you look just like her!"

"Oh, dear, I've given you some bad moments, then?"

"Yes, but you're forgiven," smiled Claudia.

Lucy laid the wedding photo down gently on the bed, as her mother got out the next one.

"This photo was taken the Christmas before I left."

Lucy looked down at a picture of her mother and Tony Ross holding their twins. They were all smiling. Claudy and Tilly looked so sweet with their big brown eyes shining under a fringe of dark hair. Lucy's heart contracted with pain as she realised the heartbreak her mother must have suffered at leaving these two beautiful children.

"You're wearing your Gemini necklace in this photo," said Lucy huskily.

"Yes. Attilio gave it to me on my first birthday after we were married," replied Claudia touching it.

"Does Dad know?"

"No, Lucy."

"Gosh, Mum, what other surprises have you got up your sleeve?"

Claudia just smiled. "It will be yours one day, Lucy. I can't give it to you now, in case you ever meet him and he recognises it. The contents of this box will be yours one day, too."

"Thank you, Mum, I'll always treasure them," she leaned over and kissed her mother's cheek.

Lucy gazed at the rest of the photos of the twins and loved the one of the boy's christening where Claudia and Colette were holding a twin each.

"These are lovely, Mum. What else is there?"

Claudia showed her daughter the locks of hair, and the boys' first pair of shoes, their first little outfits and the arm bands they had worn in the hospital. Claudia and Lucy gazed at the precious articles, eyes shimmering with tears.

While Claudia and Lucy were upstairs, Bill was down in the kitchen telling Mark and Luke their mother's sad story. The two lads listened in amazement.

"Bloody Hell!" cried Mark. "You're telling us that Mum was married to Tony Ross, and he's Lucy's dad?"

"Yes."

"No wonder Lucy's always wanted to sing!"

Luke was frowning. "Do you mean that the Mafia could still be after Mum, or have I got my wires crossed?"

"Yes, it's true, that's why Tony Ross and the Denver Brothers must never know who Lucy is."

"What a nightmare!"

"Yes, it is."

"Poor Mum."

"Don't worry, Dad, we'll look after her."

Claudia and Lucy eventually came downstairs, both red-eyed from crying. Claudia was immediately hugged by her two large sons and Lucy ran into her dad's arms.

"I'm sorry, Dad, for being so beastly, but I do love you and you'll always be my dad."

"It's alright, sweetheart, and you're still my little girl." Bill hugged her tightly.

After a rather late Sunday lunch, the men cleared away and Lucy went into the hall to phone Becky.

"Becky, it's me."

"Lucy, how's things?"

"Everything's going to be O.K. I'll tell you everything tomorrow."

"Oh, Lucy, can't you tell me anything now?"

"Well, Tony Ross's family are in the Mafia and my mum's scared to death that they'll find her and kill her for running off with me."

"Mafia!...Oh my God..how awful...your poor mum!"

"I know it's been terrible for her. I must get back to her."

"Yes, of course, I'll pick you up tomorrow at 11 O'clock."

"Thanks, Becky, bye for now."

Next Lucy spoke briefly to John Phillips, and he agreed to visit Lucy the following afternoon at her flat when she would explain everything to him. She then went back into the living room as the family had so much to talk about.

After Lucy's call, John Phillips sat deep in thought.

He lived in a beautiful town house in Mayfair. It was expensively furnished with pale green carpets, white walls, sparkling chandeliers and priceless oil paintings. The fireplaces were of white marble with realistic gas fires. The armchairs and settees were cream leather and the furniture in rich mahogany.

John Phillips had had a rather lonely life and was basically very shy. He had been an only child. His parents had died when he was very young and he had been brought up by his grandmother, who was a professional musician. She had given up her career to care for her little grandson and taken a job as a music teacher in a local grammar school in Cambridge. John got on well with his grandmother, as they both loved music. She spent many hours coaching him and gave him a safe and secure home.

When his grandmother died, he was heartbroken. She had left him everything, as his parents had done, and by the age of 23 John had been very wealthy, not to mention talented. Because of his shyness, he had put all his passion into his music. He had never been in love until he had met Lucy. Without knowing it she had swept him off his feet.

He suddenly got up out of his armchair and moved to his music room, which boasted a magnificent grand piano. He sat in front of it, his face thoughtful and ran his elegant fingers gently over the keys.

The following morning, Becky arrived at Chimneys to pick up Lucy, and was surprised to see Lucy hugging her mother tightly in the doorway. When they got into the car, Claudia waved frantically to her daughter until they were out of sight.

When Lucy had gone, Claudia went back into the house. Bill had been on the phone and he put it down and looked across at her.

"You O.K?"

"Oh, Bill, I've got my daughter back - I've got her back at last!" Bill put his arms round her and hugged her.

"And about time too," he replied gruffly.

Meanwhile, on the way back to London, Lucy told Becky her mother's story. Becky listened in amazement.

"Lucy, how frightening - no wonder you mum always looks so scared!"

"I know, she's been looking over her shoulder all these years. Every time she sees someone who looks like an Italian, she nearly dies of fright."

"How awful!"

The girls talked about Claudia and the Rossinis all morning and related the story to John Phillips in the afternoon. He listened in shocked disbelief. When he finally left he put his hands on Lucy's slim shoulders and looked into her lovely eyes.

"Lucy, I don't want you to worry. I'll look after you, and any problems you have you come straight to me."

"Yes, I will and thank you."

John Phillips walked away a very thoughtful man.

Lucy got to the theatre on Monday, her stomach churning. She was nervous about seeing the Denver Brothers now that she knew the truth. She wondered which one of them would be singing tonight - it was most annoying that she never knew which one of them was playing Rhett Butler.

She paced her dressing room nervously, her crinoline dress swishing round her ankles, until a voice came over the loudspeaker telling the cast how many minutes were left before curtain up. The characters for Act 1 Scene 1 should make their way to the wings.

When she arrived there were two Rhett Butlers waiting for her, looking dashing in their costumes, their soft, silky dark hair plastered down and their moustaches changing their faces.

The audience loved the Denver Brothers, and when they both took a bow at the curtain call, the audience went wild.

Through John Phillips, Lucy had managed to get tickets for Bill, Claudia and her two brothers on a Saturday night.

Claudia was excited and scared. She hadn't been to London since the New Year before Claudy and Tilly were born. She looked beautiful in a midnight blue dress and high-heeled gold shoes. Her hair was freshly done in a shining bob.

"You look lovely, Mum," smiled Mark.

"Terrific," grinned Luke.

The four of them were travelling down in the family car, with Bill driving. Claudia smoked nervously in the passenger seat.

They got to the theatre early, parked the car and went for a drink in a nearby wine bar. Claudia sat with her face to the wall, terrified in case someone she knew saw her. Her hands shook as she drank her wine and smoked another cigarette.

When it was time to go to the theatre, they threaded their way through the crowds. Bill handed in their tickets and they were shown to their seats, which were a few rows from the front. Bill sat next to Claudia and Mark and Luke sat on her other side. They had never been to a theatre before and looked round with interest as the seats rapidly filled up. They could sense the excitement in the air.

The lights began to dim and the music began to play. Bill nudged Claudia, whose inside was churning.

"That must be John Phillips." He pointed to the conductor. Claudia stared at the back of a blond-haired man whose arms were gently waving, baton in hand.

When the curtain rose, Bill gripped Claudia's hand. They sat spellbound as "Scarlette" began. Claudia watched the show in dazed fascination, and when Lucy began to sing, she took her breath away - she was wonderful! As soon as Rhett Butler walked onto the stage Claudia's legs began to tremble - was this Claudy or Tilly? - and when he started to sing her heart swelled. All through the musical Claudia sat transfixed. The music made her blood tingle and when Lucy sang with one of her sons, she could hardly see for the tears in her eyes. By the end of the performance, Claudia's heart was singing with joy - to see and hear Lucy with Claudy and Tilly was sensational, and tears ran down her face and the faces of many others who had been swept along in the emotional scenes.

As soon as the curtain fell, the audience began to cheer and clap, and as the curtain rose for the first curtain call people began to stand. Bill helped Claudia to her feet so that she could see Lucy, Claudy and Tilly all holding hands and smiling together. Claudia was clapping wildly, smiling and crying. Mark and Luke were whistling and shouting and Bill was beaming from ear to ear.

The curtain fell for the last time and people reluctantly started moving away.

"That was fantastic!" cried Mark.

"Our Lucy was brilliant!" grinned Luke. "Terrific!"

Bill looked down at the radiant Claudia.

"You O.K. love?"

"It was wonderful," she cried. "I didn't want it to end!"

The four of them left the theatre in high spirits and were soon on their way back to Cropwell, chatting happily about Lucy and the wonderful Denver Brothers.

"Bill!" cried Claudia. "I shall have to go and see it again and again and again!"

And she did.

FOURTEEN

LUCY AND ATTILIO 1997-1999

The next 12 months flew by and Lucy's talent was soon recognised by many. She had offers of work from all over the world, including America, but she turned them down. She was terrified of meeting her father, Tony Ross, and at the same time did not want to leave the safe and protective arms of John Phillips and the cast of "Scarlette."

She refused personal interviews but did make the occasional appearance on popular shows as a star guest. She also made some albums which were all big hits.

Her relationship with John Phillips soon developed into a natural romance and their pictures were often seen in the newspapers. They endured much teasing from the cast.

Lucy became so well-known that when she went out shopping, usually with Becky, she had to wear a disguise. Fame certainly brought its drawbacks.

Lucy and Claudia grew very close and rang each other regularly, and Claudia came down to see "Scarlette" many times, sometimes with Bill or the twins, or Colette and her family. She even came down with Maureen and Rose, who were now in their late eighties. They thought Lucy was wonderful and were so proud of her. But they still did not know that the Denver Brothers were Claudia's sons.

By the following March, the Denver Brothers' contract was almost up, and they would be going back to America. The new Rhett Butler had arrived and rehearsals had begun.

Lucy had grown very fond of her two older brothers, and felt a mixture of sadness and relief at their departure. Would she ever see them again? She wondered.

A week before the twins' departure Lucy received the shock of her life. On the Monday afternoon, after rehearsal, John Phillips beckoned to Lucy.

"What is it?" she asked anxiously, seeing the worry lines between his eyes.

"I need to speak to you, let's go up to my office."

Lucy's heart began to hammer against her ribs. What was wrong?

When they got into John's office he turned to face her and took her hands in his.

"John, what is it? You're not going away are you?"

"No, Lucy, I'm not... but there's something I have to tell you."

Lucy raised her eyebrows. "John... tell me!"

"As you know, next Saturday night we're having a party at the Hilton to say goodbye to Leo and Clay."

"Yes."

"Well... their father is coming..."

Lucy's brown eyes opened wide with shock. "You can't be serious!" she cried.

"I'm afraid so, Lucy. Tony Ross will be arriving in London on Friday morning, on a private visit. He wants to watch Clay and Leo on Friday and Saturday night. He'll then come to the party after the show, and will then fly back to America on Sunday afternoon with his sons."

Lucy went weak at the knees. "I can't believe it," she whispered.

"I'm sorry, Lucy."

"I... I... don't want to see him!" she cried in a strangled voice.

"He wants to meet you, Lucy."

"No. No. I can't. I'm too scared!"

"You have no choice, Lucy. You're the star of my show. You have to be there!" He looked down at her with troubled eyes. "You can't let me down, Lucy, or the members of the cast."

"I know, but I'm scared. He's my father and he doesn't know - but what if he guesses... I can't let him hurt my mum."

"Lucy, he doesn't know who you are, and he won't. I'll stay with you every minute, I promise."

"You won't leave me?"

"No, I promise."

"John, I'm so scared." Lucy gazed up at him, her big brown eyes dark and shimmering with tears. He pulled her shaking body into his arms, and held her close.

Lucy didn't see Becky until she got home after the evening performance. John's chauffeur had dropped her off at the door, and she flew up the stairs to the flat she still shared with her friend. The two air-stewardesses had now moved out, and Lucy's salary was sufficient to pay the rent on the flat, so that she and Becky could be on their own. Lucy was now making a lot more money and had been thinking about getting somewhere better to live, and Becky had plans to work at the theatre as Lucy's make-up artist and hairdresser - a promise that was soon to be kept.

As usual, Lucy burst through the door shouting.

"Becky, Becky, where are you?" Becky wasn't yet home and Lucy paced the floor restlessly until her friend finally came in from night-clubbing. Lucy ran up to Becky, who smiled.

"What's up, Lucy?"

"Oh, Becky, you'll never guess!"

"What is it?"

"You know you're coming to the party next week?"

"Yes," grinned Becky who was looking forward to meeting the famous Denver Brothers.

"You're going to meet Tony Ross!"

"What!"

"It's true, Bex."

"I don't believe it... you've got to be kidding!"

Lucy told her friend all that she knew.

"Oh, Lucy, you're going to meet your father!"

"I know. I'm so scared. I can't believe I've been a professional for such a short time and I will have met my father and brothers already. I thought it was going to take me a lifetime. I can't believe it's all happened so fast."

Lucy and Becky talked late into the night.

Lucy was in a state of turmoil all week. Her insides were churning and her nerves were in shreds. When her mother rang, Lucy decided not to tell her the news - she decided to confess to her after Tony Ross had gone.

Tony Ross's visit was a private one. He checked into the nearby Hilton Hotel under a false name, and there was no mention of him in the papers.

As Lucy stood in the wings on the Friday night, she took deep breaths to try and steady her nerves, knowing that Tony Ross was in the audience. After the show, she was whisked off to her flat before she had a chance to bump into him backstage. The twins were thrilled to see their father and had invited him to their dressing room.

Lucy got back to her flat still wearing her make-up. As promised, her friend was waiting up for her, and she removed the make-up from a trembling Lucy, and brushed out her hair.

On the Saturday, Lucy was so nervous that Becky went to the theatre with her. They took their dresses with them for the evening party. As it was Saturday there was a matinee and evening performance. Becky helped Lucy into her costumes, put on her make-up and generally looked after her friend. Lucy was so nervous, she was incapable of doing anything for herself.

Between the matinee and evening performance, the two girls sat in armchairs in Lucy's dressing room, and Becky went out to fetch them some food and drink.

On the way back, Becky bumped into Clay Denver. He smiled at her.

"I don't know you."

"I'm Lucy's friend, Becky."

He held out a hand. "I'm Clay Denver - nice to meet you, Becky." She shook his hand, her heart pounding.

"Thank you," she stammered.

"Coming to the party tonight?"

"Yes."

"Great. Save me a dance."

"I will."

"See you later, honey." He turned and strolled away, leaving Becky breathless. She stood and watched him - dark and handsome. Her heart suddenly sank - she would have to be careful.

She returned to the dressing room, but did not tell Lucy that she had just met the man of her dreams...

The show that night was a huge success. It was the Denvers' last performance and the audience went wild. Women in the audience were crying for Clay and Leo, and the curtain calls were endless.

Tony Ross sat in the VIP box with the manager. He was so proud of his sons. His eyes glittered as he watched Lucy. Who exactly was this beautiful, talented girl? He couldn't wait to meet her.

When the curtain calls were over, the cast all dashed off to their dressing rooms to get changed for the party. The orchestra remained in their evening dress.

Lucy and Becky helped each other get ready. Becky was almost as nervous at the thought of meeting Clay Denver again, as Lucy was at the prospect of meeting Tony Ross.

When they were ready they were met by John Phillips and taken to the Hilton Hotel by John's chauffeur. Lucy slipped her hand into John's.

"Don't leave me," she whispered.

"Never," was the quiet reply. They arrived at the hotel to find music and lights blaring and the room full or people. Many looked up as they arrived. Becky looking lovely in a dark blue chiffon, floaty dress which set off her shoulder-length blonde hair and blue eyes. Lucy looked stunning in a long, white dress, the skirt swishing round her legs. Her black hair had been swept up on top of her head, gold earrings dripped from her ears and a gold chain sparkled round her throat.

"Lucy, honey, you look like a dream," said Winnie, her black, chubby face creased with smiles.

"Thanks, Winnie."

"Lucy, you look terrific," beamed Andrea, who was wearing a gold cat-suit, a larger-than-usual ring in her little nose and glitter in her spiky hair.

Lucy looked round nervously. John stood beside her, his arm lightly round her waist. They circulated slowly, each collecting a drink. She could see Tony Ross surrounded by people and prayed her wouldn't notice her.

Eventually, to her dismay, she suddenly saw him walking slowly towards her. She froze. John took the glass out of her trembling hand, and put it on a table along with his own.

Lucy stared at Tony Ross in frozen fascination as he approached. He looked older than she expected - his black hair was streaked with silver, and he had also put on a lot of weight since he had married her mother. His neck was thicker and his shoulders were much heavier.

"Oh, God!" she thought frantically, "this man is my father - he was married to my mother... I can't believe this is happening to me..."

She looked up at him. His eyes were warm and seductive as he smiled at her, his voice was rich and mellow.

"Lucilla Lane?" he asked softly.

"Y... yes," she stammered.

"I am enchanted." He picked up her hand and kissed the back of it. She felt John's arm tighten round her waist. Tony looked across at John and smiled.

"Can I take her back to America with me, John?"

"Sorry, Tony, she's mine."

"Such a pity." He looked intently at Lucy.

"Have we met before?"

Lucy's heart leapt with fear. "No... no..." she stammered. "I am sure I would have remembered."

"You remind me of my sister."

"Your s... sister?"

"Yes. Her name is Isabella."

"Is... is... she here?"

"No. She is at home in New York. She is caring for her sick husband."

"Oh, I... I'm sorry." Lucy was beginning to shake. Sensing her terror, John spoke.

"We've got to circulate now, Tony, we'll see you later."

"Until later, Lucy." Lucy felt herself drowning in his gaze. She silently thanked God that she knew this man was her father. He was seducing her with his eyes. "You were right, Mum, you were right," she thought to herself.

John turned to Lucy and they walked towards the windows. He thought she was going to faint. As the room was so hot, many of the windows had been opened, and they made their way out onto a balcony. Wordlessly, Lucy threw herself into John's arms. He held her close and gently rubbed a hand over her slender shoulders until she stopped trembling.

"I've never been so scared in my whole life," she whispered in a choked voice. "John, don't leave me, don't ever leave me!"

He took her lovely face in his hands. "If you don't want me to leave you, I think you had better marry me." His smile was warm and loving.

"Yes," she whispered. "I will, I will!"

He pulled her into his arms and kissed her.

They eventually returned to the party, holding hands and smiling and keeping well away from Tony Ross. They danced closely together, John's hands round Lucy's slim waist and her arms round his neck, gently easing her fingers through his golden curls.

Lucy didn't notice her friend Becky with Clay Denver. The two of them spent the whole evening together, and she had been as nervous as Lucy. At the end of the evening Clay asked Becky if she would keep in touch with him after his return to America, but she made an excuse not to. Her heart sank with disappointment, but she dared not get too friendly with him in case he ever met Lucy's mother. Her loyalty to her friend had to come first.

The following Sunday, Lucy took John to Cropwell to meet her family, who were happy to hear of her forthcoming marriage. John was intrigued to meet Claudia, the woman who had been married to the famous Tony Ross, and then run away from him.

John liked Claudia immediately. She was still very pretty and sweet and nervous. He felt like a dwarf when he met Bill and his two tall sons, who towered over him like three trees! Everyone got on well and plans were made for the wedding.

Lucy told her mother about her meeting with Tony Ross.

"Oh, Lucy, he didn't guess who you were did he?" Claudia asked in alarm

"No, Mum, but he mentioned Isabella, I nearly died!"

"What did he say about her?"

"Just that I reminded him of her, and that she was in New York nursing her sick husband"

"Well, what did you think of him?"

"Charismatic, handsome and rather fat!" The two of them laughed, and hugged.

Lucy and John were married three months later on a beautiful day in June. They married in the tiny church opposite Chimneys, with Becky as bridesmaid. There were only a few people at the wedding - Lucy's family and friends and John's best man.

After the wedding and reception at the White Horse John and Lucy flew off to Paris for a short honeymoon, as Claudia had done with Tony Ross.

John and Lucy lived a happy life together in John's town house. Their life was filled with love and music and John protected Lucy as Bill had protected her mother. Lucy felt safe and relaxed.

One morning, just after their second wedding anniversary, Lucy was lying in bed - she never got up until later than her husband. On this particular morning she was lying with her eyes closed, feeling the warm sun on her face as it shone through the opened window. She suddenly became aware of John sitting on the side of the bed. She opened her eyes and smiled up at him.

"Hi!" John looked troubled. "What's wrong?"

"I've had a phone call from Tony Ross."

"Oh, no!" gasped Lucy. "What does he want?"

"He says that as you won't go to America and sing with him, he'd like to come here..."

"What...what do you mean?"

"Tony is making a video...singing songs with a variety of other well-known singers. He says if he comes to London, will you sing one song with him?"

By now Lucy was sitting up in bed, nervously tucking her hair, now cut shorter so that it skimmed her shoulders, behind her ears.

"John, I can't...I can't...I'm too scared...I don't think I could face him again."

"Well, it's up to you, darling, but just think, it might be the only time in your life you'll ever perform with him. You may regret it one day if you don't do it."

Lucy bit her lip and frowned. "Yes, that's true," she replied thoughtfully. "One day he will die, and I'll probably regret never having sung with him." She looked into her husband's calm, grey eyes. "I'll do it on one condition."

"And what's that?"

"That you will be there and stay with me every minute." John smiled and stroked her cheek with the back of his hand.

"There is no way I would let my beautiful wife be alone with Tony Ross. Of course I shall be with you."

During the next four weeks, John Phillips was in touch with Tony Ross, making arrangements for his visit to London. In the meantime Lucy was feeling more nervous, pacing the floor and unable to sleep properly. She was so scared of meeting her real father again, but at the same time was fascinated by him.

"What are we going to sing, John?"

"Tony wants to sing one of the songs from 'Scarlette'."

"Which one?"

"The song that Scarlette sings with Rhett Butler at the ball." The song was vibrant and exciting.

"I might have guessed!" retorted Lucy. "What do I have to wear?"

"Tony doesn't want full costumes in the video. He'll be wearing an evening suit, and I'd like you to wear your red dress."

"Which one?"

"The one you wore for your first audition. I fell in love with you in that dress."

Lucy laughed and slid her arms round his neck.

"O.K. I promise."

On the day of the recording, John and Lucy left early for the recording studio, as they had to get back in time for the evening performance of "Scarlette", which was still running to packed houses.

Lucy looked at herself in the mirror. The silky red dress, which showed off her bare shoulders, still fitted her well. Her dark hair was swept back in a casual, windswept style, showing up the long gold earrings falling from her ears. A gold necklace glowed against her olive skin. She took a deep breath. She was ready.

John and Lucy walked together on to the set to meet Tony Ross. He looked devastating in his evening suit, which fitted well over his now very broad shoulders and large body. His eyes and lips smiled at Lucy, as he came over and kissed her hand, Lucy started to shake.

"Lucy, my dear, there is no need to be nervous - come here." He held out his hand to her, and nodded to his conductor.

"Lucy and I will rehearse our dance to get warmed up. Please begin."

The music started to play. Tony Ross took Lucy in his arms, and they began to dance, very slowly, round the floor. Lucy was very conscious of his nearness and the warmth of his body against hers. She kept her eyes down, knowing he was watching her.

"Lucy," he said softly. She looked up into his warm, brown eyes - so like her own. "You remind me so much of my sister, Isabella, when she was young."

"How is she?"

"She is well. She is getting over the death of her husband."

"I'm sorry."

"You are very talented, Lucy. Do any of your family sing?"

Lucy's heart missed a beat.

"No. My father is a builder."

They continued to dance, slowly, Tony Ross still gazing at Lucy with narrowed eyes.

"You know, Lucy, whenever a beautiful woman performs with me I always send her a birthday card."

"You do?"

"Oh, yes, so when is your birthday?"

"The 15th of September."

"And what year were you born?" he asked softly.

"1973," she replied.

It was Tony Ross's turn to have his heart miss a beat. His arm tightened round her...

Eventually they started in earnest. It took nearly all day to do one song and dance. They sang together magnificently and danced beautifully.

"Lucy, my little one, we are so perfect together."

Lucy smiled nervously. He suddenly looked at her very seriously, his voice warm and seductive.

"Lucy. Come to America with me. I can give you the world." She looked at him, her heart pounding, mesmerised by his eyes. She remembered all that her mother had told her about him. She had to break the spell.

"I'm sorry, but I won't leave John, not even for one show." Tony Ross looked across at John Phillips.

"John, you are a very lucky man."

"I know."

Soon it was time to leave - John and Lucy to the theatre and Tony Ross and his crew to fly back to America after a short rest.

"Goodbye, Lucy." Tony Ross put his arms round Lucy and gave her a big hug. When she drew away from him, she thought she saw tears in his eyes.

"Goodbye," she replied softly and sadly.

Tony Ross watched Lucy until she was out of sight. A look of puzzlement crossed his handsome face.

When they got outside, Lucy clutched her husband's arm.

"That was the most nerve-racking day I have ever had in my life!" she cried.

"I know, but you were marvellous."

"I think he knows who I am..."

"He can't possibly know, darling."

"I've just got this feeling."

"Lucy, Tony Ross brings out emotions in everyone. He just has that way about him."

"Yes, you're probably right." But Lucy wasn't sure. She was so full of emotion she sang all the way to the theatre.

As soon as Tony Ross got back to America he contacted his best friend, Max Corder, an attorney.

"Max, I need to see you."

"What's up, Tony?"

"It's personal."

"O.K. 7 o'clock do?"

"Sure, come for dinner."

After their meal Tony and Max retired to Tony's den, where Tony poured them both a drink.

"Now, Tony, what's troubling you?"

"You've heard of the singer Lucilla Lane?"

"Sure. She's singing with you on your new video."

Tony looked across at Max. "I think she's my daughter." Max chuckled.

"So, who is the mother?"

"Claudia."

Max gasped. "You can't be serious!"

"I am."

"But what makes you so sure?"

"First of all...her likeness to Isabella...and secondly she was born on 15th September, 1973...eight months after Claudia left me...and Claudia always said that if she had a daughter she would call her Lucy after her mother...so it's possible."

"What do you want me to do?"

"Get her birth certificate from England - I think she was born there."

"I thought Claudia came to America."

"So did I at first, but she knew no-one here. I think she came here and then went back to England, where Lucy was born. She might have left me...but she wouldn't have left her sister.. she would have needed her...if she was pregnant, frightened and alone."

"What name shall I ask for?"

"Well, it won't be Rossini...or she might know who I was...try Morris...Claudia's maiden name. I want this sorted before I die."

"You're not gonna die, Tony."

"I shan't make old bones, Max. I'm very overweight, and I'm now diabetic…I have high blood pressure...and I drink too much!"

Max looked at Tony with concern in his blue eyes. He ran slim fingers through his short, grey hair. "Are you saying you wanna change your will?"

"No, but I want you to do something for me."

"What about Claudia? If you die, she could try and claim half your estate."

"No. No. She would never do that. She was never like that. Anyway she thought my family were in the Mafia...she would be too afraid to ever try to contact my family."

"What about this Lucilla Lane? What if she is your daughter - aren't you angry with Claudia?"

"No, not now. It was all my fault. I loved her, but I put my career before her happiness, and I let my family drive her away."

"What was she like, Tony? You never talk about her."

Tony Ross looked down at the drink in his hand and swirled it slowly.

"She was very beautiful, sweet and shy. She was different from all the other girls I met. When I married her she was still a virgin."

Max raised his eyebrows in disbelief.

"The only trouble with Claudia was that she was too timid. She gave up trying to learn Italian, so she isolated herself and, according to Isabella, she was so scared of my family she would spend days sitting alone in our rooms on her own. It is just as well she is not with me now, I would probably have got bored with her and if I had taken a mistress, she would have left me anyway."

"So she won't want anything from you?"

"The only thing she would want from me is her sons."

"Clay and Leo!"

"Yes, her little Claudy and Tilly."

"How are you going to do that?"

"I have something in mind. Max, just find out if Lucy is my daughter and leave the rest to me."

"O.K, Buddy."

Eventually Max Corder unfolded his long body from the chair and left.

Tony Ross sat in his armchair, a hand slowly rubbing his chin, deep in thought…

FIFTEEN

THE DEATH OF TONY ROSS 2002

It was November 2002, and New York was covered in a mantle of snow. Flakes were still gently falling as members of the public were making their way into the theatre to see the Tony Ross concert. It had been on all week and Saturday night was the last performance.

The show, as usual, was a huge success and Tony Ross, who was adored by everyone, performed as brilliantly as always. He was the most charismatic man most people had ever seen.

After the final curtain call, Tony made his way to his dressing room, wiping his brow with a clean handkerchief - it was so hot under those lights! He suddenly slowed down as his skin began to feel clammy and a cold sweat crept over his body. He got to his dressing room and collapsed.

His panic-stricken dresser ran for help and within minutes Tony Ross was in an ambulance and on his way to the nearest hospital. He had suffered a massive heart attack.

Everyone backstage was horrified and almost everyone was in tears. The Denver twins were sent for immediately and they rushed to the hospital to be with their beloved father.

Tony Ross passed away during the night with his two distraught sons at his bedside, and snowflakes softly tapping at the window.

Clay and Leo were heartbroken and wept openly. The news was released to the press and soon television and newspapers were full of the sad and shocking story.

When the news reached England it was midday on the Sunday. Claudia and Bill were at home with their two sons as the bad weather had kept Mark and Luke from their football.

Mark saw the news first on the T.V. He dashed into the kitchen to his mother.

"Mum! Mum!"

"What's up Mark?"

"It's on the news - Tony Ross - he's dead! He's had a heart attack!"

Claudia stared at him in disbelief. "Dead! You can't be serious!" Claudia and Bill ran into the living room and stared in shocked silence at the T.V.

"I can't believe it," whispered Claudia, "he's only 58."

Bill sat beside her and gripped her hand. They all stared at the T.V. listening to the newscaster giving a run-down on Tony Ross's life, and showing his distraught sons leaving the hospital. At the sight of their distress, Claudia started to cry. Bill put an arm round her shaking shoulders.

Down in London Lucy and John were busy with their twin daughters, now one year old. She and John had been overwhelmed with happiness when they had been born: two identical girls who shared their father's golden curls and blue-grey eyes.

They were all standing at the window watching the snowflakes fall. The girls, Lizbeth and Maybelle, named after John's late mother and grandmother, were smacking the glass in a vain attempt to catch the snowflakes. Lucy was laughing happily - she adored her little girls so much.

"Look well if we 'ave a white Christmas, wouldn't it be luvverly!" she laughed, mimicking Eliza Doolittle.

After her daughters were born, Lucy had taken six months off work and, with the help of a nanny, a Spanish girl called Carla, she had looked after her babies.

By the time they were six months old John had written a new musical. Lucy relinquished her role as Scarlette O'Hara and had taken on a more demanding role. Lucy was now able to spend the day with her daughters before going to the theatre in the evening. Her understudy playing her role during the Wednesday and Saturday matinees.

Lizbeth and Maybelle were now quite a handful, crawling everywhere and pulling themselves up onto their small feet, but Lucy had plenty of help from Carla, the cook, the housekeeper and Becky, who was Godmother to Lizbeth. Even the chauffeur was happy to take his share of baby-sitting!

Claudia adored her little granddaughters, and throwing caution to the wind she would often come to London for the weekend to help Lucy with them, and to give Carla some time off.

As Lucy and John were happily playing with their little girls, Carla came rushing in.

"Senor John, telefono!"

"Thank you, Carla, here take Maybelle." He passed his daughter over to Carla and went out to the hall to answer the phone.

A few minutes later he came back into the warm, spacious living room, his face pale. He looked across at Lucy.

"John, what's happened?"

He walked over to her. "Lucy, it's Tony Ross. He's had a heart attack...he died an hour ago."

Lucy gazed up at him in astonishment. "Dead? I...I...don't believe it!" she cried.

John switched on the T.V. and Lucy sat on the settee with Lizbeth on her lap, and stared at the T.V. in horror. Tears welling up in her big brown eyes.

John turned to Carla.

"Carla...can you take the girls for their dinner now?"

"Si, Senor John."

Carla took Maybelle and then came back for Lizbeth. She shut the door behind her.

John and Lucy just sat and gazed at the T.V. in shocked disbelief. Lucy, overcome with grief, cried all day.

"It's so sad!" she sobbed. "He's dead and he never knew I was his daughter. I wish I could have told him, and now it's too late!"

"At least you did meet him, Lucy, and you sang with him - you gave him that, remember, and I know how thrilled he was."

"Yes," she sobbed," and I'm so glad I did the video with him - I shall treasure it for ever, and the birthday cards he sent me afterwards and the gifts he sent when we had the girls!"

The death of Tony Ross had rocked America. Stars were interviewed and churches held memorial services. Arranagements were made for his funeral and his family flew over from Italy. New York, Tony Ross's home for many years, had a day of mourning and the newspapers and T.V. stations had a field day.

After the funeral, which had been a private one, the family went back to Tony Ross's home for a reception. During the afternoon the Denver brothers were approached by Max Corder.

"Boys, I have to sort out your father's affairs, but I can let you know that he has left almost everything to you both...."

"It's O.K. Max, we're not in any hurry," replied Claudio gruffly.

"There is just one thing. When you feel up to it could you just go through your father's effects in case there is anything I need to have?"

"Sure, Max."

Two mornings later Claudy and Tilly were sitting at the table drinking coffee after their breakfast. The Rossinis had all flown home and they were alone, apart from their staff.

"I can't believe he's gone," said Claudy sadly.

"Nor me. I feel so depressed. We lost our mother when we were small and now we've lost our father. We're only 31 and we're orphans."

They sat for some time in subdued silence.

"I want to feel close to him, let's go to his room."

"O.K."

The two of them made their way to their father's large, luxurious bedroom, and wandered aimlessly about, looking at and touching his possessions.

"I wonder why he never married again?"

"Don't know. He had plenty of offers."

"Perhaps her still loved our mother."

"I'd like to think so."

Tilly sat on the side of his father's bed and idly opened the drawer of the bedside cabinet.

"Hey, Claudy, look at this!"

"What is it?"

"Photos... there's photos here of Momma."

"Let me see."

They sat side by side looking at a pile of photos they had never seen before.

"Look, here's their wedding photos - wasn't she beautiful!"

"She sure was...and look at these, us as babies with Momma and Poppa!"

They grew excited as they stared at the pile of lovely photographs their father had kept for 30 years.

"What else is there?"

Tilly looked into the drawer and pulled out a folded piece of paper. He opened it carefully.

"What is it?"

"Their marriage certificate," cried Tilly.

"Let me see!"

"Look, they were married in London, in England! See this.... married 20th July, 1970... Atillio Giovanni Rossini..bachelor..full age... a singer... father Flavio Rossini... businessman (deceased) and Claudia Morris... spinster... full age... secretary... father Mark Morris... tour guide...(deceased)...and this witness Colette Morris must be Momma's twin sister."

"This is fantastic... is there anything else?"

Claudy looked into the drawer and pulled out an old letter with a New York postmark and dated 1973.

"What's this I wonder?" He took the letter out of the envelope and opened it out. Heads together they began to read...

Dear Atillio,

By the time you get this letter I shall be gone. Although I love you and Claudy and Tilly very much, I cannot stay here any longer. Your family hate me so much and I am unhappy and frightened whilst you are away.

They are all so cruel to me. They never speak to me and will not let me near my little boys when you are not here, and Bruno is always saying cruel things to me, and he terrifies me.

This last week, my darling, has been the last straw. I went to the nursery to try and see my little boys, and when I tried to take Claudy from your mother, because he was crying, she snatched him back from me and hit me across the face, and cut me with her ring. When she pushed me outside, I was stopped by Bruno. He put a knife to my throat and said the boys were not mine, but the 'family's' and said your family were Mafia.

The following day I went down to the nursery and there was a lock on the door, and I couldn't get in.

Atillio, I cannot take any more and I am going away. I know I cannot take my little boys with me so I am leaving them in your care. I know you will take good care of them. Tell them I love them and will think of them always. I have taken some photographs with me.

Please do not look for me, as I shall never come back. I do not want to be part of a family that is Mafia.

Please forgive me.

All my love to you and our little boys.

Claudia.

Claudy and Tilly stared at the letter in amazement and shocked disbelief.

"She didn't die," whispered Claudy in a strangled voice.

"Our family drove her away!"

"She could be still alive!" The two of them looked at each other with tear-filled eyes.

"Let's go find her!"

"Where shall we start?"

"We'll go see Aunt Isabella - she knew her."

"Good idea, come on!"

"Let's get this letter copied - we're not going to risk losing it!"

"Dad's study!"

"Come on!"

They dashed into their father's study and switched on the computer. Whilst it was warming up, Tilly rang the family chauffeur and told him to have the car ready.

With the letter safely copied, they ran downstairs and climbed into the car.

"Take us to Isabella's!" snapped Tilly.

Fifteen minutes later they drew up to the home of Isabella. They slammed the car doors as they told the chauffeur to wait, then let themselves into Isabella's home.

"Isabella!" shouted Tilly. "Where the hell are you!"

"What's the matter, boys?" Isabella was suddenly standing before them - graceful, but slightly plump. At 52 years of age she was still very pretty. Her black hair was cut in a short fashionable style, her make-up perfect. She was wearing a long black skirt and a thick black and white sweater.

Tilly glared at her and waved the copy of the letter in front of her face.

"This is what's the matter!" he shouted.

Isabella stood and read the letter. Her face paled.

"We want an explanation," said Claudy, his voice cold and hard.

"You have better come and sit down," she said quietly in her broken English.

The three of them went into the lounge and sat down.

"Why were we told she was dead?"

"It is your Poppa's wish."

"We can't believe he did this to us, and why were you cruel to her?"

Isabella looked sad. "I am sorry. I not want to be unkind to her, but I am just as afraid of Mama and Maria as Claudia. I want to be her friend, but I am too scared."

"Isabella, tell us what happened."

Isabella looked across at her nephews, who were bewildered and unhappy.

"It is true what your Momma say in her letter. She love your papa very much and it must break her heart to go away and leave you behind."

"Go on."

"Your mama, she say her sister is coming to visit her. She ask Bruno to take her to the airport to meet her. He drop her at the arrival door. She go in and he never see her again...she disappear."

"What happened?"

"Bruno, he come back and tell us what happens and Mama make him telephone a friend at the airport to see if she catch a plane. She has. She fly to New York."

"Then what?"

"Your papa, he in Australia, singing on the tour, and when he phone to speak to her we say she gone out."

"What happened when he got home?"

"Bruno, he tell him that she run away with another man."

"The lying bastard!" cried Tilly.

"What happened next," urged Claudy.

"Your papa, he is heartbroken. I try to tell him that it not true, but he not believe me."

"Then what?"

"A few days later he get the letter. Your mama, she send it to his agent. He go crazy. He try to kill Bruno. He have his hands round his throat. We have to pull him off. After that Bruno, he go away and never come back. He always in trouble, I think he end up in prison."

"Then what happened?"

"Attilio so angry with Mama and Maria - he say he never forgive them for what they have done. He never speak to them again. He angry with me too, but I tell him that Claudia is good wife and mother and that she never have gone away with another man. He not believe me because your mama she leave without luggage or money. He say his little Claudia too timid to run away on her own with nothing."

"Poor Poppa!" cried Claudy.

"What happened next?" asked Tilly, frowning.

"Your papa, he offered contract here, in America. He come here with your both and tell me I must come and look after you. He tell me to forget about boyfriends and getting married - he say it is my punishment, but I not mind - I love you both as if you are my own. And when you grow up I find good husband."

"Why did Poppa tell us she was dead?"

"It more easy that way. He not want people to know what his family has done, and he not want to frighten your mama. You know what are like the newspapers!"

"Yes, we do. Isabella, where is Momma? Do you think she is somewhere in New York?"

"No. I think she in England."

"Why?"

"When your mama leave Italy she take no luggage and no money. Atillio always leave her money in their room - it still there, so she have nothing. I think she go to her sister."

"But she was on a flight to New York!"

"*Si*, but she can fly back to England next day. Her sister, she is the air stewardess, she can arrange this."

"Yes, sure she could."

"I have another reason also."

"What's that?"

"I think she pregnant."

"Pregnant!"

"*Si*. I am sure."

"But how?"

"Simple. When your mama is pregnant with you she very sick, for many weeks. The morning after the terrible day when Mama hit her, I go up to her room. I feel sorry for her and I feel very bad. When I get to her room, I hear her be sick, very sick. The next day it is the same."

"Did you tell anyone?"

"No, I keep shut my mouth - I never tell your papa. It is a secret I keep for the sake of your mama."

"I wonder when she had the baby?"

"I can guess."

"When?"

"Atillio, he been away. He come home for Christmas and New Year, and then he go away again. She must become pregnant during this time, so the baby, it must be born no later than September. If she have more twins, then perhaps July?"

"Gee... we could have a brother or sister in England."

"Sure... we could have two! Now we have more than just Momma to look for!"

"Isabella, can you give us any more help?"

"Only one thing."

"What's that?"

"Your mama and her twin, they very close. You find her sister... you find your mama."

Claudy and Tilly stood up.

"Thanks Isabella, we sure are grateful."

"We sure are."

"Boys..."

"Yes?"

"Please, if you find your mama...tell her from me... that I am sorry... I did want to be her friend. Also tell her I think of her many times..." Isabella's eyes were filling with tears.

"We promise, Isabella." They both kissed her cheeks, marched through the door and hastily got into the car.

"Home, pal!" Tilly said to the driver.

When they got home, they told their driver to hang around. They ran into the house.

"Claudy... start packing. I'll ring the airport and book us into a hotel, and I'll ring our agent and tell him to cancel everything until we get back!"

"We could be sued!"

"Who cares... we're gonna find Momma!"

SIXTEEN

THE SEARCH FOR CLAUDIA 2002

The following morning the Denver brothers caught a flight to Heathrow. When they were incognito they always dressed differently - different clothes, glasses and wigs. They always used their real names and spoke in Italian.

They sat in the luxury of first class and talked quietly together.

"We must find out where the birth certificates are kept," said Claudy for the hundredth time.

"Yes, I know. We'll ask the concierge at the hotel, he'll know."

By the time they arrived at Heathrow, it was night time in England. They paid the exorbitant taxi fee to get to their hotel in central London - the new Hilton in Trafalgar Square. They had booked into an executive twin room, and after settling themselves in, they ordered room service, as they were both hungry.

They eventually unpacked and settled down for the night, but both found it difficult to sleep.

The following morning, after having breakfast in their room, they made they way downstairs. Tilly spoke to the concierge.

"Could you tell us where we can get a birth certificate?"

"Yes, sir. You will want the Family Record Centre in Myddleton Street. Would you like me to get you a taxi?"

"Yes, please."

The twins followed him and waited outside while he hailed them a taxi.

"Grazie (thank you)," they replied in unison.

The taxi wound it's way through the busy London Streets. Claudy and Tilly were too tense and excited to notice their surroundings. The light fall of snow England had had was already gone, and the day was cold and crisp.

As they arrived at the Family Record Centre, their hearts leapt in anticipation. They paid the driver and ran up the steps and through the glass revolving doors. As they had no luggage with them there was no bag inspection. Tilly had some hotel notepaper and a pen in his pocket.

After asking directions, they made their way through the doors leading into the search room, which was on the ground floor. They looked round at the rows and rows of steel cabinets containing hundreds of registers.

"Where the hell do we start?" groaned Tilly.

"Let's ask at this enquiry desk," suggested Claudy.

They went up to the desk and were given the same instructions as Lucy had been given years before.

"Right," said Claudy, "we want the register for 1973. July, August and September will all be in the September quarter, so we only need to look in one register."

The search room was quiet at this time of the morning, 9 a.m. and they soon found their way. They looked along the rows of registers eagerly.

"Here it is!" cried Claudy. He pulled down the register and laid it down on the long, high sloping table which stretched the length of the row of cabinets. They swiftly turned the pages to find the Rs. Claudy ran his finger down the lists of names. There was no Rossini.

"Damn!" Tilly cursed. "Now what shall we do?"

"Momma may have registered the baby under the name MORRIS."

"Good thinking!"

Eagerly they looked for the Ms but when they reached the name MORRIS they looked at each other in dismay.

"There must be hundreds here, and we don't know whether she had a girl or a boy, or where she was living."

"We must be stupid not to have realised this."

"What shall we do?"

"Why don't we find Momma's birth certificate? There might be a familiar name on it or an address we could check up on."

"O.K. Let's go for it. When do you think she was born?"

"Let's say she was Poppa's age or a bit younger. We could start in 1944 and work forwards."

"O.K."

It took a few minutes to find the cabinets which held the registers for the 1940s. The search room was already beginning to fill up.

They finally found the registers they wanted.

"I'll pull the books down," said Tilly,"and you tick off what we've done."

"O.K." Tilly passed his brother the pen and paper, and they started to search. It didn't take long and by the time they had got to the June quarter of 1946 they had found her.

"Look!" cried Claudy. "Here we are - MORRIS Claudia - mother's maiden name FORRESTER - registered in Borehamwood."

"And here's Colette - her twin sister. It's got to be the right one!"

"Come on, let's order them both." They went off and found the forms for full birth certificates and filled them in.

"Is there anything else we can do while we're here?"

"Such as?"

"Well, Isabella said if we find Colette, we'll find Momma - so why don't we look and see if we can find a marriage for Colette?"

"That's a swell idea - where shall we start?"

"Well, in 1970 she was unmarried, as she signed her name Colette Morris on Momma'a marriage certificate, so we can start in the September quarter of 1970 and just keep going."

"O.K. Come on!"

Claudy and Tilly made their way to the marriages section as another coach load of family tree enthusiasts rolled up outside. The two brothers plodded patiently through four books per year. There were a lot of Morris's but no Colette.

"What if she's never married?" puzzled Tilly.

"Don't be a killjoy - let's try a bit longer."

They eventually reached 1981, and on searching the September quarter, Claudy gasped.

"This could be her, look!" They both stared at the entry - MORRIS... Colette... HARRIS... Cropwell.

"Where the hell is Cropwell?"

"No idea."

"Shall we get it? It's the only Colette Morris we've seen."

"Sure, why not?"

Claudy filled out a form for the marriage certificate, and they queued up at the counter to pay. They had ticked the 'Collect' box on the forms, and were told they could collect the certificates in two days.

The next two days seemed like an eternity to Claudy and Tilly. Afraid of being recognised, even in disguise, they stayed in their room and had all their meals sent up. They did, however, manage to get a map of England to see where Cropwell was. Tilly looked at it in disgust.

"This Cropwell is only a tiny place, miles away from here - that marriage we ordered must be wrong!"

"Never mind, kiddo, we might be lucky yet," was his brother's hopeful reply.

The two days eventually passed and the Denvers rushed to the Family Record Centre to collect their certificates. Well-disguised they joined the inevitable queue, their insides churning with anticipation.

When they finally received the certificates, they moved away to a quiet corner and with heads together they started to read.

The first was the marriage certificate.

"It is the right one," said Claudy. "Look, her father's name is Mark Morris.... tour guide.... deceased, same as on Momma's. Colette married a schoolteacher called Simon Harris."

They turned to their mother's birth certificate.

"Here we go," whispered Claudy, "Claudia Morris... born...

6th June 1946... father Mark Morris... tour guide... mother Lucy Ann Morris nee Forrester."

They suddenly turned and looked at each other, eyes alight.

"Lucy!"

"Holy shit! Do you think Lucilla Lane could be our sister?"

"She could be - she's a singer and Poppa said she reminded him of Isabella!"

"I can't believe it!"

"Come on, let's go and find her birth certificate!" They dashed over to the birth section and pulled down the September quarter of 1973 again. Claudy ran his finger down the neatly typed page of MORRISs until he came to Lucy - registered in Cropwell.

"Cropwell again! It's got to be her!"

"How can we be sure?"

"I know. Let's find Lucy's marriage to John Phillips."

"Good idea, come on!"

"They made their way to the marriage section, talking excitedly.

"When did they get married?"

"After we left 'Scarlette'."

"Let's start 1998." They did. They found the marriage of John Phillips and Lucy Morris in the June quarter in Cropwell.

"Bingo!" cried Claudy, beaming all over his face.

They ordered the birth and marriage of Lucy.

"I don't think I can wait two days for those certificates. I want to see Lucy now and she can tell us where Momma is."

"Let's make sure we're right first - and don't forget, Lucy may not know we're her brothers - she might get a terrible shock - she might not even know that Poppa was her father."

"True, but it could be the other way - she may know the truth and be as scared as Momma is."

"Hell, what are we going to say to her?"

In a state of euphoria they returned to their hotel and spent the next two days going over and over what they were going to say to their sister, Lucy and when were they going to find their mother?

The two days dragged by. It was a wet Saturday morning - but the spirits of the Denver brothers were high.

They stood restlessly in the queue, their hearts pounding, their hands shaking. The certificates collected at last, they opened them with trembling hands.

They gazed at Lucy's birth certificate - their eyes filling with tears.

"She put Poppa's name on it...look!"

"Bless you, Momma, bless you," whispered Claudy. It was there in black and white... Lucy Morris... born 15th September, 1973... father Atillio Giovanni Rossini...a singer...mother... Claudia Morris... birth registered by mother... Claudia Morris, May Cottage, Bishops Fell, Nr. Cropwell.

"Lucy," whispered Claudy,"our beautiful, talented, little sister! Dear Lucy!"

"It's too good to be true," replied his shaken brother.

"Let's look at Lucy's marriage... here we go."

They gazed at it together...10th June, 1998... John Phillips... full age... bachelor... musical director and Lucy Morris... full age... a singer... spinster... father... William Harris... a builder.

"Momma's got another man!" cried Claudy in horror. Tilly swallowed hard.

"Yes. It didn't take long, but I guess it was sure to happen she's very beautiful."

"Just a minute... Colette married a Harris! Perhaps two sisters married two brothers?"

"Do you think Momma committed bigamy?"

"They're probably not married."

"True, but Momma took his name."

"When are we going to see Lucy? Shall we go now?"

"No, she's performing tonight... we can't give her a shock just before a performance - we'll go and see her in the morning."

"I wonder if we could get into Lucy's show tonight, so that we could see her?"

"No, chance, but we might get into the matinee."

"She doesn't do matinees since she had her daughters."
"Daughters, of course... she had twins as well."
"Our family is growing by the minute."
"It sure is. Roll on tomorrow!"

SEVENTEEN

FINAL CURTAIN 2002

Sunday morning woke to a clear sky, and a warm sun whose weak rays lit up the thick frost which had turned London into a fairy grotto.

"It's a beautiful day," smiled Claudy, running slender fingers through his smooth dark hair as he looked out of their hotel bedroom window.

"Let's hope it stays beautiful - I feel sick with nerves."

"So do I. I don't know how I managed to get any sleep last night."

"Nor me."

"What time shall we go?"

"Not too early. John and Lucy will have had a late night, they probably won't be up yet."

"Yes, but they've got two little girls - I bet they'll wake up early."

"What if we get there at 10 o'clock?"

"Yep, that sounds about right."

Totally unaware of the events that were about to happen, the Phillips household was a hive of activity. Lucy had been very subdued after the death of Tony Ross; she had taken the death of her real father very badly, but this particular weekend Bill and Claudia had come up for a visit and Lucy and her mother had had time to chat about the amazing man who had entered their lives.

By 10 o'clock John and Lucy were up and about with their two little girls, and Bill and Claudia were happily playing with their little grandchildren, along with Becky who was a regular visitor. Carla was having the day off and enjoying a lie-in. The cook and housekeeper were busy, one making beds and tidying up and the other in the kitchen preparing a Sunday lunch for them all. John Phillips's chauffeur-cum-butler was resting in his room down in the basement.

At 10 o'clock the front door bell rang. It was answered by the housekeeper.

Lucy was in the living room chatting to Becky when the housekeeper came in.

"Lucy, there are two gentelmen to see you."

"Who are they?"

"I don't know."

"I'll go and see them," she smiled leaving the room and making her way into the hall. She looked up to see two young men standing there in winter coats with collars turned up, long dark hair and glasses.

"How can I help you," she asked quietly.

Claudy and Tilly took off their wigs and glasses and smiled.

"Hi, Lucy."

"Clay, Leo!" she gasped, putting a hand up to her throat. "W...what are you doing here?"

"We've come to see you, Lucy, because we've discovered that you are our sister."

"Oh, My God!" cried Lucy. "What do you want?"

John, who had appeared in the hallway looked on in amazement.

"We want to see our mother, Lucy."

"No,no. You can't see her!" cried Lucy.

"We don't want to hurt her, Lucy. Our family are not a part of the Mafia, it was all lies to frighten her away. There's no need for you to be afraid."

John Phillips crept quietly into the living room.

Lucy, nervously pushing her hair behind her ears with trembling fingers looked at them in astonishment.

"How... how... did you find out?" She stared at them with tear-filled eyes.

Suddenly Claudy and Tilly looked down the hall and gasped. Lucy turned.

The Denver brothers stared at the woman now standing by the living room door - a middle-aged woman with short gold and silver hair, big blue eyes brimming with tears, and wearing a fluffy white sweater and blue jeans.

"Momma?"

"Claudy... Tilly!" cried Claudia," my boys!"

The next moment, she found herself in the arms of her long-lost sons. She slipped an arm round each of their waists, and burst into tears.

John put an arm round his shell-shocked wife, led her into the living room and shut the door.

"What's going on?" asked Bill, puzzled.

"Bill, it's Claudia's sons - they've come looking for her, but don't worry."

"Good God, how did they find her?"

"I've no idea - but it's so soon after the death of Tony Ross, he may have had something to do with it."

"But the Mafia?" urged Bill.

"They're not Mafia," added Lucy wiping her eyes, "they said so."

"Thank God for that!" sighed Bill. Becky looked across at Lucy.

"Clay and Leo... they really are here?"

"Yes." Becky's heart missed a beat.

Out in the hallway Claudia and her sons were hugging and kissing each other.

"Oh, Claudy, Tilly... I thought I'd lost you for ever. I'm so sorry I left you - it broke my heart... please forgive me."

"It's O.K. Momma, we understand."

Claudia's voice was breaking with emotion. "How... how did you find me?"

"We found your letter," replied Tilly, looking adoringly at his mother.

"My letter? You mean your father *kept* it?"

"Yes."

"I didn't want to hurt him, I'm so sorry."

"It's O.K. Momma, we understand. We're real glad we found you."

"So am I. This is wonderful!"

"And Momma, we're not Mafia - Bruno was lying. Our family just wanted to drive you away, and they did."

"How do you know all this?"

Claudy and Tilly told Claudia about their visit to Isabella and all she had told them.

"Isabella...how is she?"

"She's just fine. She said to tell you how sorry she was and that she would like to have been your friend. She brought us up and was very good to us. She says she often thinks of you."

"I'm so glad. I wanted to be her friend, too. It's all so sad."

They continued talking excitedly. Soon a radiant Claudia entered the living room with her two happy sons.

"Bill, I'd like to introduce you to Claudy and Tilly."

Bill shook their hands. "Nice to meet you. I've heard a lot about you both."

"You have?"

"Oh, yes, and Claudia and I came to see you in 'Scarlette'." Their faces lit up as they looked at their mother.

"You came to see us?"

"Yes, a number of times."

"Oh, Momma!" Claudia found herself being hugged by her sons again.

Suddenly John came in with a tray of glasses and a bottle of champagne.

"I think it's time we had a celebration," he smiled. There was a cheer from everyone.

As John was pouring the drinks, Tilly looked down to see Maybelle tugging his trousers.

"Hey, look at this, I got a little niece!"

"Me, too!" cried Claudy, picking up Lizbeth.

Suddenly the room was filled with joyous laughter and everyone was chatting madly to each other. John informed the cook that there would be two extra for dinner.

The Denver brothers stayed all day, as there was so much to talk about and the catching up of many lost years. Claudy and Tilly were overjoyed at finding their mother and sister.

During the evening, Claudy rang Isabella to tell her the good news. He then turned to his mother.

"Momma, say hello to Isabella..."

"Isabella... it's Claudia here."

"Claudia, my dear, how wonderful! I am so happy... your sons they find you."

"Isabella, I want to thank you for all your help and for looking after my boys for me."

"It is nothing. I am happy to do this for you, and Claudia, I am sorry for what happen to you. I wish very much to be your friend, but Mama..."

"I understand, Isabella. I realised that you were just as scared as I was."

"Now we can be friends, yes?"

"Of course we can, that would be lovely."

"And you come to America and see me, yes?"

"I'd love to, Isabella."

The two women chatted happily while Claudy renewed his friendship with the blushing Becky, and Lucy and Bill were in conversation with Tilly.

Later that evening, Bill spoke to the twins.

"How long can you both stay in England?"

"I think we can risk another week," replied Tilly.

"Would you both like to come home with us to Cropwell? You can meet your twin brothers and your Aunt Colette."

"That would be great, Bill, thanks."

"We'll be going after breakfast tomorrow, we can pick you up from your hotel."

"Cheers, Bill."

Bill rang his sons at home and told them the news. They were delighted to be meeting their famous brothers at last.

They all talked late into the night, all unwilling to be parted. Eventually the Denvers left for their hotel. They hugged and kissed Claudia.

"We love you, Momma."

"And I love you both very much," she whispered."This has been the happiest day of my life."

The lads then gave Lucy a big hug.

"Goodnight, beautiful sister."

"And goodnight to my two lovely brothers, and Tilly, mind where you put your hands!"

Tilly laughed heartily.

"Sorry about that, Lucy."

John's chauffeur took the Denvers back to their hotel. Becky stayed overnight with the family, her heart singing with happiness after meeting Claudy again.

Claudia found it difficult to sleep after such a wonderful, exciting day.

"I've never seen you look so happy," said Bill gently.

"Oh, Bill, I feel as if a great burden has fallen from my shoulders. I feel as if I have been released from a prison of guilt."

"It's been an unforgettable day, and I like your boys - I think they are great."

"Thank you, Bill." She put her arms round him and hugged him, and his big hand gently stroked her hair.

Lucy was so excited after the day's events she chatted non-stop when she got to bed, and although her husband was listening, an idea was stirring in his brain.

The Denvers were also having difficulty getting to sleep.

"What a fantastic day!"

"Isn't Momma wonderful!"

"Yep, she sure is. She's beautiful and sweet - how Poppa could have been so stupid as to let her go I'll never know."

"Nor me, and Lucy is a doll. I still can't believe she's our sister!"

"I know, it's all like a dream."

"I liked Bill, too, he's a great guy."

"He sure is. And the size of him! He could have been a basketball player back home."

"I wonder if our brothers are as tall?" mused Tilly.

"Isn't it just crazy! We lose Poppa and all of a sudden we've got a mother, a sister, two nieces and two half-brothers. It's unbelievable," exclaimed Claudy.

"I can't sleep! Let's call the family. They should all be at home about now."

"Good idea we'll ring Max and then the others in Italy." Claudy picked up the phone.

The following morning everyone was up early. The Denvers packed quickly and had breakfast in their room.

In the meantime, Claudia and Bill were also packed and had breakfast. They kissed Lucy and her family goodbye and set off happily to pick up Claudy and Tilly.

Meanwhile up in Cropwell, Mark and Luke were getting ready for their parents' arrival along with their two older brothers. Mark and Luke's girlfriends had been round on the Sunday afternoon to make sure the house was clean and tidy, and the guest bedroom was ready for the Denvers. As Mark and Luke worked for their father they had been able to take the day off work on this special Monday. Their girlfriends had to go to work, but had promised to call round early in the evening. They, too, were looking forward to meeting the famous duo.

During the morning, Colette, who was also greatly excited, went to Chimneys. Her son, Martin now 16, and her husband Simon were at school, and would be arriving at 4 o'clock.

Colette was looking forward to seeing her nephews again. She was striding up and down the living room, restlessly, and kept going to the window.

On the drive to Cropwell, Claudia chatted excitedly to her sons, still unable to believe that they had found her. Bill was grinning from ear to ear at the sound of the three happy people in his car.

At 12 o'clock the car drew up to Chimneys, and Mark and Luke hurried out to meet their parents and brothers, and to help with the luggage. As they got out of the car Bill introduced the two sets of brothers. Mark and Luke looked down, rather shyly, at their two small, dapper Italian brothers with American accents.

"Nice to meet you." They all shook hands.

Claudy and Tilly looked up at their two huge brothers - 6'4" of muscle with the blond hair and blue eyes of their mother.

"Hi. fellas - it's great to meet you. You sure are a surprise!" They all grinned at each other.

Suddenly Colette stepped out, and the Denvers stared at her in amazement, then at each other.

"I'm Colette, it's lovely to see you both again."

"Jeez!" exclaimed Tilly, "you sure are like Momma!" he kissed her on both cheeks.

"That sure was a great trick you pulled, getting Momma away from Italy," added Claudy to his aunt.

"Well, things were pretty desperate at the time - and we did miss you both," she added.

Eventually they made their way into the house. Claudia showed her sons round Chimneys and they put their luggage in the guest room.

When they got downstairs, Colette, efficient as always, provided them all with tasty filled rolls and coffee.

"You sure have a swell house, Bill - and you did all this?"

"Yes, it was an old coaching inn at one time, and I converted it into a house."

"You should be here in the summer," smiled Claudia. "The view in the garden is beautiful."

While everyone was chatting, Bill booked a table in the restaurant at the White Horse for the evening.

During the afternoon, Claudia showed her sons the photos and the little treasures she had brought with her from Italy. They were deeply touched at the sight of their locks of hair and tiny clothes. They both hugged their mother, and more tears were shed.

The day soon became hectic with the arrival of Simon and Martin, the girlfriends of Mark and Luke and the very elderly Maureen and Rose who were simply astonished at learning the truth about Claudia, and were tickled pink to meet the famous duo.

Everyone was talking madly and Claudy and Tilly were almost speechless as they were surrounded by such wonderful people.

In the evening they all walked over to the White Horse where they all had a wonderful meal, bottles of champagne, and drunk numerous toasts.

The rest of the week flew by. Claudia and Bill showed Claudy and Tilly round Cropwell and Bishops Fell and were shown the tiny cottage where their mother had hidden herself away. The Denvers felt deeply sorry for their mother and all the sadness she had suffered at the hands of their family.

"If I ever find Uncle Bruno, I'll kill him with my bare hands," Tilly hissed at his brother.

"Not if I find him first," was the grim reply.

A couple of evenings during the week Mark and Luke took their brothers out on the town. Claudy and Tilly loved the olde-worlde pubs and the friendly people of Cropwell. The four brothers, although totally different, got on well together.

The end of the week arrived much too quickly, and everyone was reluctant to be parted.

Arrangements were made for Bill, Claudia and their family to fly to America for Christmas and the New Year. They would stay at the Rossini home in New York and meet up with Isabella and friends of the Denvers.

Bill and Claudia took them to the airport. Claudia tearfully hugged and kissed her sons.

"We'll see you soon, Momma."

"Yes, I can't wait. Take care my darlings."

The three of them hugged and kissed and the boys shook Bill's hand.

"Thanks for a great week, Bill."

"It's been a pleasure, boys, Come and see us whenever you wish, you will always be welcome."

Claudia and Bill stood and waved as Claudy and Tilly made their way into the departure lounge.

Claudia was silent all the way home, and when she got in she walked up to the window overlooking the back garden, and watched the winter sun dipping behind the dark trees at the bottom of the garden.

Bill went up behind her and slid his arms round her waist.

"You O.K. love?"

"I feel as though I've just lived through a wonderful dream. I've got my boys back, Bill, I've got them back. I can hardly believe it's true.

Bill smiled and kissed the top of her head.

Claudia was safe and happy at last.

EPILOGUE

By the time Claudy and Tilly returned to New York it was already December, and they frantically began, between engagements, making preparations for Christmas.

In Cropwell Claudia and Bill were also busy. They both had to renew their passports which were now out of date, and Colette helped Claudia to buy Christmas presents for Claudy, Tilly and Isabella, and buy some new clothes.

Now that Claudia was widowed she and Bill were able to marry without any fuss. The ceremony took place on a Sunday so that Lucy and her family could be there. It was a quiet wedding at the tiny church opposite Chimneys, with just the family and the faithful Maureen and Rose, now in their nineties, the adopted grandmothers of Claudia's children.

The days were joyous and hectic and the phone was busy with Claudia and her sons ringing each other regularly.

The day before Christmas Eve Claudia, Bill, Mark and Luke drove up to London to stay the night with Lucy before they all flew off to New York. Carla was busy packing for Maybelle and Lizbeth and looking forward to going to America with the family. Her dark, pretty face was all smiles and her plump little body bouncing as she bobbed happily about.

Becky arrived, invited by Claudy was also joining the party. Although Becky had had many boyfriends, Claudy was the only man she had ever wanted.

Lucy and her family were only staying for a couple of days as they had to back for their show. She and Becky had been giggling together.

"Oh, Bex, just to think - if you marry Claudy, you'll be my sister-in-law! Isn't it exciting!"

"Keep your fingers crossed that he asks me!" Becky had laughed happily.

On Christmas Eve they all set off for Gatwick airport. The security was now very strict after the terrible bombing of the twin towers the year before. They all settled comfortably into first class.

With the time change, they arrived in New York on the morning of Christmas Eve. They were met by limousines which took them to the Rossini mansion, which stood proudly under a mantle of snow. It had been well-prepared for it's visitors - with a huge Christmas tree, decorations and gifts. Cots, high-chairs and push-chairs were in readiness for Lucy's children, and huge baskets of flowers had been placed in the rooms prepared for Claudia, Lucy and Becky.

Everyone was happy and excited as they arrived. Claudy, Tilly and Isabella came out to meet them, large snowflakes falling gently on their faces.

Claudia's sons hugged and kissed her, then she found herself being greeted by Isabella.

"Claudia, my dear, it's so good to see you!" Isabella hugged her and kissed her cheeks.

"Isabella, how lovely - and you are still just as beautiful!" smiled Claudia happily.

They all made their way into the warmth of the house, Isabella's arm linked with Claudia's.

"I so much want to meet your daughter!" cried Isabella.

"Lucy," called Claudia, "come and meet Isabella." Lucy walked up to her aunt, smiling.

"Oh, Lucy, you are so beautiful, and you look like your papa!" cried Isabella.

"Aunt Isabella, it's lovely to meet you, and thank you so much for helping Claudy and Tilly to find us."

"It is nothing. I happy to do this." Isabella suddenly spotted Lizbeth and Maybelle, and rushed over to them with a cry of delight. Claudia and Lucy looked at each other and smiled.

After unpacking, everyone spent the day chatting and laughing, eating and drinking. Friends came round to meet Claudia and her family and Max Corder called in, looking rather pleased with himself.

Christmas Day was perfect. Warmth, luxury and joy inside, snow sparkling outside. Everyone had slept well in their huge, luxurious rooms. Lucy and John had been given Tony Ross's room, and Lucy had been fascinated to be in the room her real father had slept in, and she touched his belongings with tear-filled eyes.

The Denvers and their two younger brothers had laughed and joked together and had all gone to bed a little drunk.

Christmas dinner was held at lunch time in a magnificent dining room. All the family plus Max Corder, sat round the huge table to a wonderful meal and expensive wines. Everyone was relaxed and happy after opening their Christmas presents, and having an excellent meal.

When the last of the dishes had been cleared away and the coffee had been served and more bottles of wine, Tilly spoke.

"Now, folks, you've all met Max, who was our father's closest friend and his attorney. At his request we have invited him here, as he wishes to speak to you all. Over to you, Max."

Everyone looked at each other, a little puzzled as the thin, grey-haired Max looked round at them all and began to speak. He looked at Claudia.

"First of all, Claudia, Tony asked me to tell you how deeply sorry he was at the way you were treated by his family. He blames himself for being so blind and selfish, and hopes that you will forgive him."

There was a stirring round the table, and the air became tense.

Claudia looked across at him with tear-filled eyes.

"Of course," she replied softly.

Max continued. "Some time ago Tony and I were discussing his will, and I asked him if he wanted to leave you anything. He said to me that all you would want from him was your sons, and I'm very happy, and I know that he would be too, that they've been returned to you."

"Yes, that's true," she whispered as Claudy and Tilly, who were sitting either side of her, each took one of her hands. Max looked at her sons.

"Clay and Leo - I now congratulate you both for finding your mother, and so quickly, too."

"How did he know we were going to find her?" demanded Tilly.

"We left you enough clues," smiled Max.

"You mean the letter and those documents were put there for us to find?"

"Yes. They were removed from your father's safe and put into the drawer."

"But we may have never found her without the help of Isabella. What if we had got stuck?"

"Then I was to give you a nudge in the right direction."

"But if he knew where Momma was, why weren't we told?"

"Your father thought it would be a good challenge for you, and that you would get more pleasure by looking for her yourselves."

"The sly old fox!" they cried in unison.

Max smiled and then turned to Lucy. "Lucy, now it is your turn. Tony guessed you may have been his daughter when you sang with him for his video. He asked me to thank you from the bottom of his heart, you made him very happy."

"Why didn't he say something?" asked Lucy in a choked voice.

"He wouldn't risk it Lucy, because he didn't want to distress your mother. He knew how frightened she had been, and probably still was. He guessed she had made a new life for herself, and he wasn't prepared to shock or upset her. He would liked to have been a proper father to you when he knew who you were - but felt it was his punishment. He only had himself to blame for never having known you."

Lucy's lips began to tremble as tears trickled down her lovely face. She gripped her husband's hand.

"Tony asked me to give you some gifts," Max added as he picked up a briefcase from beside his chair. He opened it and took out a photograph of Tony Ross in a gold frame. Across was written, in his flowery handwriting, "To my Lucy - all my love - Papa Attilio." He handed it to Lucy.

"Oh!" she gasped. "Thank you." She gazed at the photo with misty eyes, her hands shaking.

Max then passed to Lucy a velvet covered box. She took it and opened it slowly. She gasped as she lifted the lid to reveal, lying on white satin, a priceless set of jewellery. There was a thick gold necklace with a large diamond dropper and a pair of matching earrings. Attached to the satin was a card which read: "Lucy, wear these for me. Papa."

"I don't know what to say!" cried Lucy, tears now pouring down her face. John put an arm round her shoulders and passed her a clean handkerchief. The box was passed round the table for everyone to see.

When Lucy had calmed down, Max then passed her some personal gifts, given to her father by Claudia when they were married. There was a set of cufflinks with musical notes engraved in the gold and a dark blue silk tie with a matching design. Max smiled at Lucy.

"Tony thought you could give them to your son if you ever have one."

Lucy took the gifts from Max. "I'll treasure these always, thank you."

Max coughed. "Lucy, Tony also asked me to give these gifts to you for his little granddaughters, they're for their 18th birthday." He passed Lucy two small jewellery boxes. Inside each one was a beautiful gold bracelet with a note saying "Happy birthday, love Nanno (Grandad) Attilio."

Lucy was speechless with emotion.

Max turned to Claudia again. "Claudia, I know this has all been rather emotional, but there is one more thing."

"Yes?"

"Before his death, Tony recorded a new song called 'I'm Sorry'. It will be released next week and you're to have all the royalties."

He passed her a small box with a tape inside and a card which read. "Claudia - this is for you, Cara, with love, Attilio."

Claudia sat speechless, also unable to speak.

Bill suddenly stood up and looked round the table as he spoke. "I never knew Tony Ross, but to me it seems he was a pretty good guy." He raised his glass. "To Tony Ross."

They all looked at Bill with shining eyes.

"Hear, hear!"

"To Tony Ross!"

They all raised their glasses and drank a toast to the dead singer.

They then all sat round the table talking and bombarding Max with questions.

It was an unforgettable Christmas.

The following year Claudia and Bill went to Italy and spent two weeks with Attilio's brothers. Flavio and Sergio, and their families. Claudia and Paula were overjoyed to see each other again after so many years, and kept in touch regularly.

Isabella came over to Cropwell many times. She and Claudia became the best of friends, keeping in touch and visiting each other for the rest of their lives.

The following Christmas, Lucy gave birth to a son. He was named Attilio John William, and was the image of his famous grandfather.

Claudy and Tilly, who adored their mother, both bought houses in Cropwell and spent many years of their lives in England to be near her.

Claudy married Becky, much to everyone's delight and Tilly married Andrea ('pet monkey') who eventually got rid of the ring in her nose, grew her hair and looked very pretty. Becky and Andrea both had a boy and a girl.

Over the years, Claudia grew in confidence and radiated happiness. She coped with the fame of being the wife of Tony

Ross and she grew warm and friendly, becoming popular with the inhabitants of Cropwell at last.

With the permission of Claudia and her family John Phillips wrote a new musical based on the life of Tony Ross, which was an instant success.

He called it "DANGEROUS SONG".